Meet Just William

Richmal Crompton, who wrote the original William stories, was born in Lancashire in 1890. The first story about William Brown appeared in *Home* magazine in 1919, and the first collection of William stories was published in book form three years later. In all, thirty-eight William books were published, the last one in 1970, after Richmal Crompton's death.

Martin Jarvis, who has adapted the stories in this book for younger readers, first discovered *Just William* when he was nine years old. He made his first adaptation of a William story for BBC radio in 1973 and since then his broadcast readings have become classics in their own right. BBC Worldwide has released nearly a hundred William stories on audio and for these international bestsellers Martin has received a Gold Disk and a British Talkies Award. An award-winning actor, Martin has also appeared in numerous stage plays, television series and films.

Titles in the Meet Just William *series*

Meet Just William

Adapted from
Richmal Crompton's original
stories by Martin Jarvis

Illustrated by Tony Ross

Three
books
in one!

MACMILLAN CHILDREN'S BOOKS

William's Birthday and Other Stories first published 1999 by
Macmillan Children's Books
William and the Hidden Treasure and Other Stories first published 1999 by
Macmillan Children's Books
William's Wonderful Plan and Other Stories first published 1999 by
Macmillan Children's Books

This edition published 2008 by Macmillan Children's Books
a division of Macmillan Publishers Limited
20 New Wharf Road, London N1 9RR
Basingstoke and Oxford
www.panmacmillan.com

Associated companies throughout the world

ISBN: 978-0-330-45343-1

3 5 7 9 8 6 4 2

A CIP catalogue record for this book is available from
the British Library.

Typeset by SX composing DTP, Rayleigh, Essex
Printed and bound in Great Britain by Mackays of Chatham plc, Kent

Contents

Dear Reader

Ullo. I'm William Brown. Spect you've heard of me an' my dog Jumble cause we're jolly famous on account of all the adventures wot me an' my friends the Outlaws have.

Me an' the Outlaws try an' avoid our famlies cause they don' unnerstan' us. Specially my big brother Robert an' my rotten sister Ethel. She's awful. An' my parents are really hartless. Y'know, my father stops my pocket-money for no reason at all, an' my mother never lets me keep pet rats or anythin'.

It's jolly hard bein' an Outlaw an' havin' adventures when no one unnerstan's you, I can tell you.

You can read all about me, if you like, in this excitin' an' speshul new collexion of all my fav'rite stories. I hope you have a jolly gud time readin' 'em.

Yours truly

William Brown

William's Birthday

and Other Stories

Contents

William's Birthday

It was William's birthday, but, in spite of that, his spirit was gloomy and overcast. He hadn't got Jumble, his beloved mongrel, and a birthday without Jumble was, in William's eyes, a hollow mockery of a birthday.

Jumble had hurt his foot in a rabbit trap, and had been treated for it at home, till William's well-meaning but mistaken ministrations had caused the vet to advise Jumble's removal to his own establishment.

William had indignantly protested, but his family was adamant. And when the question of his birthday celebration was broached, feeling was still high on both sides.

"I'd like a dog for my birthday present," said William.

"You've got a dog," said his mother.

"I shan't have when you an' that man have killed it between you," said William. "He puts on their bandages so tight that their calculations stop flowin' an' that's jus' the same as stranglin' 'em."

"Nonsense, William!"

"Anyway, I want a dog for my birthday present. I'm sick of not havin' a dog. I want another dog. I want two more dogs."

"Nonsense! Of course you can't have another dog."

"I said two more dogs."

"You can't have two more dogs."

"Well, anyway, I needn't go to the dancing-class on my birthday."

The dancing-class was at present the bane of William's life. It took place on Wednesday afternoons – William's half-holiday – and it was an ever-present and burning grievance to him.

He was looking forward to his birthday chiefly because he took for granted that he would be given a holiday from the dancing-class. But it turned out that there, too, Fate was against him.

Of course he must go to the dancing-class, said Mrs Brown. It was only an hour, and it was a most expensive course, and she'd promised that he shouldn't miss a single lesson because Mrs Beauchamp said that he was very slow and clumsy and she really hadn't wanted to take him.

To William it seemed the worst that could

possibly happen to him. But it wasn't. When he heard that Ethel's admirer, Mr Dewar, was coming to tea on his birthday, his indignation rose to boiling point.

"But it's my birthday. I don't want *him* here on my birthday."

William had a deeply rooted objection to Mr Dewar. Mr Dewar had an off-hand, facetious manner which William had disliked from his first meeting with him.

William awoke on the morning of his birthday, still in a mood of unmelting resentment.

He went downstairs morosely to receive his presents.

His mother's present to him was a dozen new handkerchiefs with his initials upon each, his father's a new leather pencil-case. William thanked them with a manner of cynical aloofness of which he was rather proud.

"Now, William," said his mother anxiously, "you'll go to the dancing-class nicely this afternoon, won't you?"

"I'll go the way I gen'rally go to things. I've only got one way of goin' anywhere. I don't know whether it's nice or not."

This brilliant repartee cheered him considerably. But still: no Jumble; a dancing class; *that* man to tea. Gloom closed over him again. Mrs Brown was still looking at him anxiously. She had an uneasy suspicion that he meant to play truant from the dancing-class.

When she saw him in his hat and coat after lunch she said again, "William, you *are* going to the dancing-class, aren't you?"

William walked past her with a short laugh that was wild and reckless and daredevil and bitter and sardonic. It was, in short, a very good laugh, and he was proud of it.

Then he swaggered down the drive, and very ostentatiously turned off in the opposite direction to the direction of his dancing-class. He walked on slowly for some time and then turned and retraced his steps with furtive swiftness.

To do so he had to pass the gate of his home,

but he meant to do this in the ditch so that his mother, who might be still anxiously watching the road for the reassuring sight of his return, should be denied the satisfaction of it.

He could not resist, however, peeping cautiously out of the ditch when he reached the gate, to see if she were watching for him. There was no sign of her, but there was something else that made William rise to his feet, his eyes and mouth wide open with amazement.

There, tied to a tree in the drive near the front door, were two young collies, little more than pups. Two dogs. He'd asked his family for two dogs and here they were. Two dogs. He could hardly believe his eyes.

His heart swelled with gratitude and affection for his family. How he'd misjudged them! Thinking they didn't care two pins about his birthday, and here they'd got him the two dogs he'd asked for as a surprise, without saying anything to him about it. Just put them there for him to find.

His heart still swelling with love and gratitude, he went up the drive. The church clock
struck the hour. He'd only just be in time for the
dancing-class now, even if he ran all the way.

His mother had wanted him to be in time
for the dancing-class and the sight of the two
dogs had touched his heart so deeply that he
wanted to do something in return, to please
his mother.

He'd hurry off to the dancing-class at once,
and wait till he came back to thank them for
the dogs.

He stooped down, undid the two leads from the tree, and ran off again down the drive. The two dogs leapt joyfully beside him.

The smaller collie began to direct his energies to burrowing in the ditches, and the larger one to squeezing through the hedge, where he found himself, to his surprise, in a field of sheep.

He did not know that they were sheep. It was his first day in the country. He had only that morning left a London shop. But dim instincts began to stir in him.

William, watching with mingled consternation and delight, saw him round up the sheep in the field and begin to drive them pell-mell through the hedge into the road; then, hurrying, snapping, barking, drive the whole jostling perturbed flock of them down the road towards William's house.

William stood and watched the proceedings. The delight it afforded him was tempered with apprehension.

The collie had now made his way into a third field, in search of recruits, while his main army waited for him meekly in the road. William hastily decided to dissociate himself from the proceedings entirely. Better to let one of his dogs go than risk losing both . . .

He hurried on to the dancing-class. Near the front door he tied the collie to a tree with the lead, and entered a room where a lot of little boys – most of whom William disliked intensely – were brushing their hair and changing their shoes.

At last a tinkly little bell rang, and they made their way to the large room where the dancing-class was held. From an opposite door was issuing a bevy of little girls, dressed in fairy-like frills, with white socks and dancing-shoes.

There followed an attendant army of mothers and nurses who had been divesting them of stockings and shoes and outdoor garments.

William greeted these fairy-like beings with his most hideous grimace. The one he disliked most of all (a haughty beauty with auburn curls) was given him as a partner.

"*Need* I have William?" she pleaded. "He's so *awful.*"

"I'm not," said William. "I'm no more awful than her."

"Have him for a few minutes, dear," said Mrs Beauchamp, who was tall and majestic and almost incredibly sinuous, "and then I'll let you have someone else."

The dancing-class proceeded on its normal course. William glanced at the clock and sighed. Only five minutes gone. A whole hour of it – and on his birthday. His *birthday*. Even the thought of his two new dogs did not quite wipe out *that* grievance.

"Please may I stop having William now? He's doing the steps all wrong."

William defended himself with spirit.

"I'm doin' 'em right. It's her what's doin' 'em wrong."

Mrs Beauchamp stopped them and gave William another partner – a little girl with untidy hair and a roguish smile. She was a partner more to William's liking, and the dance developed into a competition as to who could tread more often on the other's feet.

It was, of course, a pastime unworthy of a famous Indian Chief, but it was better than dancing. He confided in her.

"It's my birthday today, and I've had two dogs given me."

"*Oo!* Lucky!"

"An' I've got one already, so that makes three. Three dogs I've got."

"Oo, I say! Have you got 'em here?"

"I only brought one. It's in the garden tied to a tree near the door."

"Oo, I'm goin' to look at it when we get round to the window!"

They edged to the window, and the little girl glanced out with interest, and stood, suddenly paralysed with horror, her mouth and eyes wide open. But almost immediately her vocal powers returned to her.

"*Look!*" she said. "Oh, *look!*"

They all crowded to the window.

The collie had escaped from his lead and found his way into the little girls' dressing-room.

There he had collected the stockings, shoes, and navy-blue knickers that lay about and brought them all out on to the lawn, where he was happily engaged in worrying them.

Remnants lay everywhere about him. He was tossing up into the air one leg of a pair of navy-blue knickers. Around him the air was thick with wool and fluff. Bits of unravelled stockings, with here and there a dismembered hat, lay about on the lawn in glorious confusion.

He was having the time of his life.

After a moment's frozen horror the whole dancing-class – little girls, little boys, nurses, mothers, and dancing-mistress – surged out on to the lawn.

The collie saw them coming and leapt up playfully, half a pair of knickers hanging out of one corner of his mouth, and a stocking out of the other.

They bore down upon him in a crowd. He wagged his tail in delight. All these people coming to play with him!

He entered into the spirit of the game at once and leapt off to the shrubbery, followed by all these jolly people. A glorious game! The best fun he'd had for weeks . . .

Meanwhile William was making his way

quietly homeward. They'd say it was all his fault, of course, but he'd learnt by experience that it was best to get as far as possible away from the scene of a crime . . .

He turned the bend in the road that brought his own house in sight, and there he stood as if turned suddenly to stone. He'd forgotten the other dog.

The front garden was a sea of sheep. They covered drive, grass and flower beds. They even stood on the steps that led to the front door. The overflow filled the road outside.

Behind them was the other collie pup, running to and fro, crowding them up still more closely, pursuing truants and bringing them back to the fold.

Having collected the sheep, his instinct had told him to bring them to his master. His master was, of course, the man who had brought him from the shop, not the boy who had taken him for a walk. His master was in this house. He had brought the sheep to his master . . .

His master was, in fact, with Ethel in the drawing-room. Mrs Brown was out and was not expected back till tea-time.

Mr Dewar had not yet told Ethel about the two collies he had brought for her. She'd said last week that she "adored" collies, and he'd decided to bring her a couple of them. He meant to introduce the subject quite carelessly, at the right moment.

And so, when she told him that he seemed to understand her better than any other man she'd ever met (she said this to all her admirers in turn), he said to her quite casually, "Oh! By the way, I forgot to mention it but I just bought a little present – or rather presents – for you this afternoon. They're in the drive."

Ethel's face lit up with pleasure and interest.

"Oh, how perfectly sweet of you," she said.

"Have a look at them, and see if you like them."

She walked over to the window. He remained in his armchair, watching the back

15

of her Botticelli neck, lounging at his ease –
the gracious, all-providing male. She looked
out. Sheep – hundreds and thousands of sheep
– filled the drive, the lawn, the steps, the road
outside.

"Well," said Mr Dewar, "do you like
them?"

She raised a hand to her head.

"What are they for?" she said faintly.

"Pets," said Mr Dewar.

"*Pets!*" she screamed. "I've nowhere to

keep them. I've nothing to feed them on."

"Oh, they only want a few dog biscuits."

"*Dog* biscuits?"

Ethel stared at them wildly for another second, then collapsed on to the nearest chair in hysterics.

Mrs Brown had returned home. Mrs Brown had had literally to fight her way to the front door through a tightly packed mass of sheep.

Mr Dewar was wildly apologetic. He couldn't think what had happened. He couldn't think where the sheep had come from.

The other dog arrived at the same moment as a crowd of indignant farmers demanding their sheep. It still had a knicker hanging out of one corner of its mouth and a stocking out of the other.

William was nowhere to be seen.

William came home about half an hour later. There were no signs of Mr Dewar, or the dogs, or the sheep. Ethel and Mrs Brown were in the drawing-room.

"I shall never speak to him again," Ethel was saying. "I don't care whether it was his fault or not. I've told him never to come to the house again."

"I don't think he'd dare to when your father's seen the state the grass is in. It looks like a ploughed field."

"As if I'd want hundreds of *sheep* like that," said Ethel, still confusing what Mr Dewar had meant to do with what he had actually done. "*Pets* indeed!"

"And Mrs Beauchamp's just rung up about the other dog," went on Mrs Brown. "It evidently followed William to the dancing-class and tore up some stockings and things there. I don't see how she can blame us for that. She really was very rude about it. I don't think I shall let William go to any more of her dancing-classes."

William sat listening with an expressionless face, but his heart was singing within him. No more dancing classes . . . that man never coming to the house any more. A glorious birthday – except for one thing, of course.

But just then the housemaid came into the room.

"Please, 'm, it's the man from the vet with Master William's dog. He says he's quite all right now."

William leapt from the room, and he and Jumble fell upon each other ecstatically in the hall. The minute he saw Jumble, William knew that he could never have endured to have any other dog.

"I'll take him for a little walk. I bet he wants one."

The joy of walking along the road again, with his beloved Jumble at his heels. William's heart was full of dreamy content.

He'd got Jumble back. That man was never coming to the house any more.

He wasn't going to any more dancing-classes.

It was the nicest birthday he'd ever had in his life.

The Christmas Truce

It was Hubert Lane's mother's idea that the Outlaws versus Hubert Laneites feud should be abolished.

"Christmas, you know," she said vaguely to William's mother, "the season of peace and good will. If they don't bury the hatchet at this season, they never will. It's so absurd for them to go on like this. Think how much *happier* they'd be if they were *friends*."

Mrs Brown murmured, "Er – yes," and Mrs Lane continued, "I've thought out how to do it. If you'll invite Hubie to Willie's party, we'll *insist* on his coming, and we'll invite Willie to Hubie's and you *insist* on his coming, and then it will be all right. They'll have got to know each other, and, I'm sure, have learnt to love each other."

Mrs Brown said, "Er – yes" again, because she couldn't think of anything else to say, and so the matter was settled.

When it was broached to William, he was speechless with horror.

"*Him?*" he exploded fiercely, when at last the power of speech returned to him. "Ask *him* to my Christmas party? I'd sooner not have a Christmas party at all than ask *him* to it. *Him!* Well then, I jolly well won't have a party at all."

But William's tempestuous fury was as usual of no avail against his mother's gentle firmness.

"William," she said. "I've promised."

She sent an invitation to Hubert Lane and to Bertie Franks (Hubert's friend and lieutenant) and to Hubert's other friends, and they all accepted in their best copperplate handwriting.

William and his Outlaws went about sunk deep in gloom.

"If it wasn't for the trifle an' the crackers," said William darkly, "I wouldn't have had it at all – not with *him*."

His mood grew darker and darker as the day approached. The prospect of the end of the feud brought no glow of joy to the Outlaws' hearts. Without the Hubert Lane feud, life would be dull indeed.

The Outlaws and their supporters – as arranged – arrived first, and stood round William like a bodyguard, awaiting the arrival of the Hubert Laneites.

They wore perfectly blank expressions, prepared to meet the Hubert Laneites in whatever guise they presented themselves. And the guise in which they ultimately presented themselves was worse than the Outlaws' worst fears.

They advanced upon their host with an oily friendliness that was nauseating. They winked at each other openly. They said, "Thanks *so* much for asking us, William. It was ripping of you. Oh, I say . . . what *topping* decorations!"

And they nudged each other and sniggered.

Mrs Brown, of course, was deceived by their show of friendliness.

"There, William," she whispered triumphantly, "I knew it would be all right. I'm sure you'll be the *greatest* friends after this. His mother *said* he was a nice little boy."

William did not reply to this because there wasn't anything he could trust himself to say.

They went in to tea.

"Oh, I say, how *ripping*! How *topping*!" said the Hubert Laneites gushingly to Mrs

Brown, nudging each other and sniggering whenever her eye was turned away from them.

Once Hubert looked at William and made his most challenging grimace, turning immediately to Mrs Brown to say with an ingratiating smile, "It's a simply topping party, Mrs Brown, and it's awfully nice of you to ask us."

Mrs Brown beamed at him and said, "It's so nice to *have* you, Hubert," and the other Hubert Laneites sniggered.

William kept his hands in his pockets with such violence that one of them went right through the lining.

But the crowning catastrophe happened when they pulled the crackers.

Hubert went up to William and said, "See what I've got out of a cracker, William," and held up a ring that sent a squirt of water into William's face.

The Hubert Laneites went into paroxysms of silent laughter. Hubert was all smirking contrition.

"I say, I'm so sorry, William, I'd no idea that it would do that. I just got it out of one of the crackers. I say, I'm so sorry, William."

It was evident to everyone but Mrs Brown that the ring had not come out of a cracker, but had been carefully brought by Hubert in order to play this trick on William.

William was wiping water out of his eyes and ears.

"It's quite all right, dear," said Mrs Brown. "It was *quite* an accident, we all saw. They shouldn't have such nasty things in crackers, but it wasn't your fault. Tell him that you don't mind a bit, William."

But William hastily left the room.

The rest of the party passed off uneventfully. The Hubert Laneites said goodbye at the end with nauseous gratitude and went sniggering down the drive.

"*There*, William!" said Mrs Brown as she shut the door. "I knew it would be all right. They were so grateful and they enjoyed it *so* much and you're *quite* friends now, aren't you?"

But William was already upstairs in his bedroom, pummelling his bolster with such energy that he burst his collar open.

During the days that intervened between William's party and Hubert Lane's party, the Hubert Laneites kept carefully out of the way of the Outlaws. Yet the Outlaws felt uneasily that something was brewing.

"We've gotter do somethin' to them at their

party, same as they did to us at ours," said Ginger firmly.

"Yes, but what can we do?" said William. "We can't start fightin' 'em. We've promised not to. An' – an' there's nothin' else we *can* do. Jus' wait, jus' *wait* till their party's over."

"But they'll never forget that water squirt," said Ginger mournfully.

"Unless we do somethin' back," said Douglas.

"What can we do in *their* house, with them watchin' us all the time?" said Henry.

"We mus' jus' *think*," said William. "There's four days an' we'll think hard."

But the day of Hubert's party arrived, and they'd thought of nothing.

They met in the old barn in the morning to arrange their plan of action, but none of them could think of any plan of action to arrange.

William walked slowly and draggingly through the village on his way home to lunch. His mother had told him to stop at the baker's with an order for her, and it was a sign of his intense depression that he remembered to do it.

He entered the baker's shop. It seemed to be full of people. Then he suddenly realised that the mountainous lady just in front of him was Mrs Lane.

She was talking in a loud voice to a friend.

"Yes, Hubie's party is this afternoon. We're having William Brown and his friends. To put a stop to that silly quarrel that's gone on so long. Hubie's so lovable that I simply can't think how anyone could quarrel with him.

But of course it will be all right after today.

"We're having a Father Christmas, you know. Bates, our gardener, is going to be the Father Christmas and give out presents. I've given Hubie three pounds to get some *really* nice presents for it to celebrate the ending of the feud."

William waited his turn, gave his message, and went home for lunch.

Immediately after lunch, he made his way to Bates's cottage, which stood on the road at the end of the Lanes' garden.

William approached the cottage with great circumspection, looking around to make sure that none of the Hubert Laneites was in sight.

He opened the gate, walked up the path, and knocked at the door, standing poised on one foot ready to turn to flee should Bates, recognising him – and remembering some of his former exploits in his kitchen garden – attack him on sight.

He heaved a sigh of relief, however, when Bates opened the door. It was clear that Bates did not recognise him – he merely received him with an ungracious scowl.

"Well?" said Bates. "What d'you want?"

William assumed an ingratiating smile, the smile of a boy who has every right to demand admittance to the cottage.

"I say," he said, with a fairly good imitation of the Hubert Laneites' most patronising manner, "you've got the Father Christmas things here, haven't you?"

The ungraciousness of Bates's scowl did not relax. He had been pestered to death over the Father Christmas things.

He took for granted that William was one of the Hubert Laneites, coming once more to "muss up" his bag of parcels, and take one out, or put one in, or snigger over them, as they'd been doing every day for the last week.

"Yes," he said, "I've got the things 'ere an' they're all right, so there's no call to start upsettin' of 'em again. I've had enough of you comin' in an' mussin' the place up."

"I only wanted to count them, and make

sure that we've got the right number," said William with an oily friendliness that was worthy of Hubert himself.

"All right, go in an' count 'em. I tell you, I'm sick of the whole lot of you, I am." And Bates waved him irascibly into the back parlour.

William entered, and threw a quick glance out of the window. Yes, Ginger was there, as they had arranged he should be, hovering near the shed where the apples were sorted.

Then he looked round the room. A red cloak and hood and white beard were spread out on the sofa, and on the hearthrug lay a sackful of small parcels.

William fell on his knees and began to make pretence of counting the parcels. Suddenly, he looked up and gazed out of the window.

"I say!" he said. "There's a boy taking your apples."

Bates leapt to the window. There, upon the roof of the shed, was Ginger, with an arm through the open window, obviously in the act of purloining apples.

With a yell of fury, Bates sprang to the door and down the path towards the shed. Left alone, William turned his attention quickly to the sack. It contained parcels, each one labelled and named.

He had to act quickly. He had no time to investigate. He had to act solely upon his suspicions and his knowledge of the characters of Hubert and his friends.

Quickly, he began to change the labels of the little parcels. Just as he was fastening the last one, Bates returned, hot and breathless, having failed to catch the nimble Ginger.

"Now you clear out," he said. "I'm sick of the lot of you."

Smiling the patronising smile of a Laneite, William took a hurried departure, and ran home as quickly as he could to change.

The Hubert Laneites received the Outlaws with even more nauseous friendliness than they had shown at William's house.

It was evident, however, from the way they sniggered and nudged each other that they had some plan prepared. William felt anxious. Suppose that the plot they had so obviously prepared had nothing to do with the Father Christmas . . .

They went into the hall after tea, and Mrs Lane said roguishly, "Now, boys, I've got a visitor for you."

Immediately, Bates, inadequately disguised as Father Christmas and looking fiercely resentful of the whole proceedings, entered with his sack.

The Hubert Laneites sniggered delightedly.

This was evidently the crowning moment of the afternoon. Bates took the parcels out one by one, announcing the name on each label.

The first said "William".

The Hubert Laneites watched him go up to receive it in paroxysms of silent mirth. William took it and opened it wearing a sphinx-like expression.

It was the most magnificent mouth organ that he had ever seen. The mouths of the Hubert Laneites dropped in horror and amazement. It was evidently the present that Hubert had destined for himself.

Bates called out Hubert's name. Hubert, his mouth still hanging open with horror and amazement, went to receive his parcel.

It contained a short pencil with a shield and rubber, of the sort that can be purchased for a penny or twopence. He went back to his seat, blinking.

He examined his label. It bore his name. He examined William's label. It bore William's name. There was no mistake about it.

William was thanking Mrs Lane effusively for his present. "Yes, dear," she was saying, "I'm so glad you like it. I haven't had time to look at them, but I told Hubie to get nice things."

Hubert opened his mouth to protest, and then shut it again. He was beaten and he knew it.

He couldn't very well tell his mother that he'd spent the bulk of the money on the presents for himself and his particular friends, and had spent only a few coppers on the Outlaws' presents. He couldn't think what had happened.

Meanwhile, the presentation was going on. Bertie Franks' present was a ruler that could not have cost more than a penny, and Ginger's was a magnificent electric torch.

Bertie stared at the torch with an expression that would have done credit to a tragic mask, and Ginger hastened to establish permanent right to his prize by going up to thank Mrs Lane for it.

"Yes, it's lovely, dear," she said. "I told Hubie to get nice things."

Douglas's present was a splendid penknife, and Henry's a fountain pen, while the corresponding presents for the Hubert Laneites were an indiarubber and a notebook.

The Hubert Laneites watched their presents passing into their enemies' hands with expressions of helpless agony.

But Douglas's parcel had more than a penknife in it. It had a little bunch of imitation flowers with an indiarubber bulb attached, and a tiny label saying, "Show this to William and press the rubber thing."

Douglas took it to Hubert. Hubert knew what it was, of course, for he had bought it, but he was paralysed with horror at the whole situation.

"Look, Hubert," said Douglas.

A fountain of ink caught Hubert neatly in the eye. Douglas was all surprise and contrition.

"I'm so sorry, Hubert," he said. "I'd no idea

38

that it was going to do that. I've just got it out of my parcel and I'd no idea that it was going to do that. I'm so sorry, Mrs Lane. I'd no idea that it was going to do that."

"Of course you hadn't, dear," said Mrs Lane. "It's Hubie's own fault for buying a thing like that. It's very foolish of him indeed."

Hubert wiped the ink out of his eyes and sputtered helplessly.

Then William discovered that it was time to go.

"Thank you so much for our lovely presents, Hubert," he said, politely. "We've had a *lovely* time."

And Hubert, under his mother's eye, smiled a green and sickly smile.

The Outlaws marched triumphantly down the road, brandishing their spoils. William was playing on his mouth organ, Ginger was flashing his electric torch, Henry was waving his fountain pen, and Douglas was slashing at the hedge with his penknife.

Occasionally they turned round to see if

their enemies were pursuing them, but the
Hubert Laneites were too broken in spirit to
enter into open hostilities just then.

As they walked, the Outlaws raised a wild
and inharmonious paean of triumph.

And at that moment over the telephone,
Mrs Lane was saying to Mrs Brown, "Yes,
dear, it's been a *complete* success. They're the
greatest friends now. I'm sure it's been a
Christmas that they'll all remember all their
lives."

William Leads a Better Life

If you go far enough back, it was William's form master who was responsible for the whole thing.

Mr Strong had set for homework more French than it was convenient for William to learn. Who would waste the precious hours of a summer evening over French verbs? Certainly not William.

In the morning, however, things somehow seemed different. William lay in bed and considered the matter.

"Mother, I don't think I feel quite well enough to go to school this morning," he called faintly.

Mrs Brown entered the room looking distressed. She smoothed his pillow.

"Poor little boy," she said tenderly. "Where's the pain?"

"All over," said William, playing for safety.

But the patient's father, when summoned, was having none of it.

"You'd better get up as quickly as you can. You'll be late for school. And doubtless they'll know how to deal with *that*."

They did know how to deal with that. They knew too how to deal with William's complete ignorance on the subject of French verbs.

He went home to lunch embittered and disillusioned with life. On the way, Ginger, Henry and Douglas began to discuss the history lesson.

The history master had given them a graphic account of the life of St Francis of Assisi. William had paid little attention, but Ginger remembered it all. William began to follow the discussion.

"Yes, but why'd he do it?" he said.

"Well, he jus' got kind of fed up with things, an' he had visions an' things, an' he took some things of his father's to sell to get money to start it—"

"*Crumbs!* Wasn't his father mad?"

"Yes, but that di'n't matter. He was a saint, was Saint Francis, so he could sell his father's things if he liked, an' he 'n' his frien's took the money and got long sort of clothes, an' went an' lived away in a little house by themselves, an' he use' ter preach to animals, an' to people, an' call everythin' 'brother' an' 'sister' an' they cooked all their own stuff to eat an'—"

"Jolly fine it sounds," said William enviously. "An' did their people let 'em?"

"They couldn't stop 'em," said Ginger. "An' Francis – he was the head one – an' the others all called themselves Franciscans, an' they built churches an' things."

They had reached the gate of William's house now, and William turned in slowly.

Lunch increased still further William's grievances. No one enquired after his health, though he tried to look pale and ill, and refused a second helping of rice pudding with a meaningful, "No thank you, not today. I would if I felt all right, thank you very much."

Even that elicited no anxious enquiries.

No one, thought William, as he finished up the rice pudding in secret in the larder afterwards, no one else in the world, surely, had such a callous family. It would just serve them right if he went off like St Francis and never came back.

He met Henry and Ginger and Douglas again as usual on the way to afternoon school.

"I've been thinkin' a lot about that saint man. I'd a lot sooner be a saint than keep goin' to school an' learnin' things like French verbs without any *sense* in them. I'd much sooner be a saint, wun't you?"

The other Outlaws looked doubtful.

"They wun't let us," said Henry.

"They can't stop us bein' saints," said William piously, "an' doin' good, an' preachin' – not if we have visions. An' I feel as if I could have visions quite easy."

The Outlaws had slackened their pace.

"What'd we have to do first?" said Ginger.

"Sell some of our fathers' things to get money," said William firmly. "Then we find a place, an' get the right sort of clothes to wear – sort of long things—"

"Dressing-gowns'd do," said Douglas.

"All right," said William.

"Where'll we live?" said Henry.

"We oughter build a place, but till we've

45

built it, we can live in the old barn," said William.

"An what'll we be called? We can't be the Outlaws now we're saints, I s'pose?"

"What were they called?"

"Franciscans . . . After Francis – he was the head one."

"Well, if there's goin' to be any head one," said William, "I'm goin' to be him."

None of them denied to William the position of leader. It was his by right. He had always led, and he was a leader they were proud to follow.

"Well, they just put 'cans' on to the end of his name," said Henry. "Franciscans. So we'll be Williamcans—"

"Sounds kind of funny," said Ginger dubiously.

"I think it sounds jolly fine," said William proudly.

The first meeting of the "Williamcans" was held directly after breakfast the next morning, on Saturday, in the old barn. They had all left notes, dictated by William, on their bedroom mantelpieces, announcing that they were now saints and had left home for ever.

They inspected the possessions that they had looted from their unsuspecting fathers: William had appropriated a pair of slippers, Douglas an inkstand, Ginger had two ties, and Henry a pair of gloves.

They looked at their spoils with proud satisfaction.

"We'd better not put on our saint robes yet
– not till we've been down to the village to
sell the things. Then we'll put 'em on an'
start preachin' an' things. An', remember –
from now on, we've gotter call each other
'Saint' an' call everythin' else 'brother' or
'sister'."

"*Everything?*"

"Yes – *he* did – the other man did."

"Yes, but William—"

"You've gotter call me St William now,
Ginger."

"All right. You call me St Ginger."

"All right, I'm goin' to, St Ginger—"

"St William."

"All right."

"Well, where you goin' to sell the slippers?"

"*Brother* slippers," corrected William.
"Well, I'm goin' to sell brother slippers at Mr
Marsh's, if he'll buy 'em."

"And I'll take brother ties along too," said
Ginger. "And Henry take brother gloves and
Douglas, brother inkstand."

"Sister inkstand," said Douglas. "William said—"

"St William," corrected William patiently.

"Well, St William said we could call things brother or sister, and my inkstand's going to be sister."

"Swank," said St Ginger severely. "Always wanted to be diff'rent from other people."

Mr Marsh kept a second-hand shop at the end of the village. He refused to allow them more than sixpence each.

"Mean!" exploded St William indignantly, as soon as they'd emerged from Mr Marsh's dingy little sanctum.

"I suppose now we're saints," said St Ginger piously, "that we've gotter forgive folks what wrong us like that."

"Huh! I'm not going to be that sort of saint," said St William firmly.

Back at the barn, they donned their dressing-gowns.

"Now what do we do first?" said St Ginger.

"Preachin' to animals," said William. "Let's go across to Jenks's farm an' try on them."

They crept rather cautiously into the farm-yard.

"I'll do brother cows," said St William, "an' St Ginger do brother pigs, an' St Douglas do brother goats, an' St Henry do sister hens."

They approached their various audiences. Ginger leant over the pigsty. Then he turned to William, who was already striking an attitude before his congregation of cows, and said, "I say, what've I gotter *say* to 'em?"

At that moment, brother goat, being approached too nearly by St Douglas, butted the saintly stomach, and St Douglas sat down suddenly and heavily.

Brother goat, evidently enjoying this form of entertainment, returned to the charge. St Douglas fled, to the accompaniment of an uproarious farmyard commotion.

Farmer Jenks appeared, and, seeing his old

enemies, the Outlaws, actually within his precincts, he uttered a yell of fury and darted down upon them.

The saints fled swiftly, St Douglas holding up his too-flowing robe as he went. Brother goat had given St Douglas a good start, and he reached the barn first.

"Well," said St William, panting, "I've *finished* with preachin' to animals. They must have changed a good bit since *his* time. That's all *I* can say."

"Well, what'll we do *now*?" said Ginger.

51

"I should almost think it's time for dinner," said William.

It was decided that Douglas and Henry should go down to the village to purchase provisions for the meal. It was decided also that they should go in their dressing-gowns.

For their midday meal, the two saints purchased a large bag of chocolate creams, another of bull's-eyes, and, to form the more solid part of the meal, four cream buns.

Ginger and William were sitting comfortably in the old barn when the two emissaries returned.

"*We've* had a nice time!" exploded St Henry. "All the boys in the place runnin' after us an' shoutin' at us. Douglas has tore his robe and I've fallen in the mud in mine."

"Well, they've gotter last you all the rest of your life," said St William, "so you oughter take more care of 'em," and he added with more interest, "What've you got for dinner?"

When they had eaten, they rested for a short time from their labours.

"I s'pose they *know* now at home that we've gone for good," said Henry with a sigh.

Ginger looked out of the little window anxiously.

"Yes. I only hope to goodness they won't come an' try to fetch us back," he said.

But he need not have troubled. Each family thought that the missing member was having lunch with one of the others and felt no anxiety, only a great relief.

And none of the notes upon the mantelpieces had been found.

"What'll we do *now*?" said William.

"*They* built a church," said Ginger.

"Well, come on," said William, "let's see 'f we can find any stones lyin' about."

They wandered down the road. They still wore their dressing-gowns, but they wore them with a sheepish air.

Fortunately, the road was deserted. They looked up and down, then St Ginger gave a yell of triumph.

The road was being mended, and there by

the roadside, among other materials, lay a little heap of bricks. Moreover, the bricks were unattended. It was the workman's dinner hour.

"Crumbs!" said the Williamcans in delight.

They fell upon the bricks and bore them off in triumph. Soon they had a pile of them just outside the barn where they had resolved to build the church.

But as they paid their last visit for bricks, they met a little crowd of other children, who burst into loud, jeering cries.

"Look at 'em . . . dear little girlies . . . wearin' nice long pinnies . . . oh my! Oh, *don'* they look sweet? Hello, little darlin's!"

William flung aside his saintly robe and fought with the leader. The other saints fought with the others. The saints, smaller in number and size than the other side, most decidedly got the best of it, though not without many casualties.

The other side took to its heels.

St William picked his robe up from the mud

and began to put it on. "Don' see much *sense* in wearin' these things," he said.

"You ought to have *preached* to 'em, not fought 'em," said Ginger severely.

"Well, I bet *he* wun't have preached to 'em if they'd started makin' fun of him. He'd've fought 'em all right."

"No, he wun't," said Ginger firmly. "He di'n't believe in fightin'."

"Well, anyway," said William, "let's get a move on buildin' that church."

They returned to the field.

But the workman had also returned from his dinner hour.

With lurid oaths he tracked them down, and came upon the saints just as they had laboriously laid the first row of bricks for the first wall. He burst upon them with fury.

They did not stay to argue. They fled. Henry cast aside his splendid robe of multi-coloured bath towelling into a ditch to accelerate his flight. The workman tired first, after throwing a brick at their retreating forms.

The Williamcans gathered together dejectedly in the barn.

"Seems to me," said William, "it's a *wearin'* kind of life."

It was cold. It had begun to rain.

"Brother rain," said Ginger brightly.

"Yes, an' I should think it's about sister tea-time," said William. "An' what we goin' to buy it – her – with? How're we goin' to get money?"

They thought deeply for a minute.

"Well," said William at last, voicing the

opinion of the whole order, "I'm jus' about sick of bein' a saint."

The rest looked relieved.

"Yes, I've had *enough*," said William. "There's no *sense* in it. An' I'm almost dyin' of cold and hunger an' I'm goin' home."

They set off homeward, cold and wet and bruised and very hungry. The saintly repast, though enjoyable at the time, had proved singularly unsustaining.

But their troubles were not over.

As they went through the village, they

stopped in front of Mr Marsh's shop window.

There in the very middle were William's father's slippers, Douglas's father's inkstand, Ginger's father's tie, and Henry's father's gloves – all marked at one shilling.

The hearts of the Williamcans stood still. The thought of their fathers seeing their prized possessions reposing in Mr Marsh's window, marked one shilling, was a horrid one.

It had not seemed to matter this morning. This morning, they were leaving their homes for ever. It did seem to matter this evening. This evening, they were returning to their homes.

They entered the shop and demanded them. Mr Marsh was adamant. In the end, Henry fetched his sixpence, William a treasured penknife, Ginger a compass, and Douglas a broken steam engine, and their paternal possessions were handed back.

They went home, dejectedly through the rain.

William discovered with relief that his

father had not yet come home. He found his note unopened still upon the mantelpiece. He tore it up. He tidied himself superficially. He went downstairs.

"Had a nice day, dear?" said his mother.

He disdained to answer the question.

"There's just an hour before tea," she went on. "Hadn't you better be doing your home-work, dear?"

He considered. One might as well drink of tragedy to the very dregs while one was about it. It would be a rotten ending to a rotten day.

Besides, there was no doubt about it, Mr Strong was going to make himself very disagreeable indeed if he didn't know those French verbs for Monday. He might as well . . .

If he'd had any idea how rotten it was being a saint, he jolly well wouldn't have wasted a whole Saturday over it. He took down a French grammar and sat down moodily before it, without troubling to put it the right way up.

William and the Musician

William sat on the crest of the hill, his chin cupped in his hands. He surveyed the expanse of country that swept out before him and, as he surveyed it, he became the owner of all the land and houses as far as he could see.

Finding the confines even of England too cramping for him, he became the ruler of the whole world.

He made sweeping and imperious gestures with his right arm – gestures that sent his servants on missions to the farthest ends of the earth.

It was at this point that William realised he

was not alone. A small man had climbed the hill and now sat watching him with interest. Near the small man was a large pack.

"Well, did you catch it?" said the small man pleasantly, as William turned to meet his eye.

"Catch what?" said William.

"The mosquito. I thought you got him that last grab."

"Yes, I got him all right," said William coldly. He swept his arm around in another circle and added, "All that land belongs to me. It's mine as far as you can see."

The man had a brown, humorous but sad face. He looked impressed.

"But you're under age, of course. I suppose you have a guardian or an agent of some sort to manage it for you."

"Oh yes," said William. "Oh yes, I have a guardian or agent all right."

"Your parents are both dead, of course?" the man said.

"Oh yes," said William. "Oh yes, my parents are both dead all right."

"And where do you live?"

The most imposing house within sight was the Hall.

William pointed to it.

"I live there," he said.

As a matter of fact, the Hall was rather in the public eye at present. Mr Bott (of Bott's Sauce) lived there, and Mrs Bott had recently given a staggering subscription to the rebuilding of Marleigh Cottage Hospital.

The result of this was that the Chairman

of the Hospital, Lord Faversham, was coming down from London to attend a party at the Hall to which the entire neighbourhood – including the Browns – was invited, and which was to assure for ever Mrs Bott's place among the neighbouring aristocracy.

William had heard nothing else mentioned in the village for days past.

"I'm giving a large party there next Friday," he said nonchalantly. "Lord Faversham's coming to it, and a lot more dukes and earls and things."

William suddenly caught sight of a little dog lying on the ground behind the pack, fast asleep.

"I say," he said, "is that your dog?"

"Yes," said the little man, "it's Toby. Wake up, Toby. Show the gentleman what you can do, Toby."

Toby woke up and showed the gentleman what he could do. He could walk on his hind legs and dance and shoulder a stick and pace up and down like a sentry. William watched him ecstatically.

"I say! I've never *seen* such a clever dog!"

"Never *was* such a dog," said the little man. "But do people want him? No. Punch and Judy's out of date, they say. I don't know what the world's coming to."

William's eyes opened still further.

"You got a Punch and Judy show?" he said.

The man nodded and pointed to his pack on which the faded letters "Signor Manelli" could be faintly seen.

"Yes," he said. "Same as my father before me, though my father never had a dog like Toby."

He was actually an Italian, he said, and had come to England with his father and mother when he was only a few weeks old.

He had never been out of England since, but his ambition was to make enough money to go back to Italy to his father's people. It was an ambition, however, that he had almost given up hope of fulfilling.

"Well, I *like* Punch and Judy," said William, "and if—"

The little man interrupted him, his soft, brown eyes shining. "Listen," he said, "this party you're giving on Friday. Couldn't you engage us for that? I promise that we'd give you our best performance."

"Er – yes," said William flatly. "Yes, of course."

"I'll come then? What time does the party begin?"

"Er – three o'clock," said William, struggling with a nightmarish feeling of horror. "But I'm afraid – you see – I mean—"

"I promise you I won't disappoint your guests. You won't regret it. I thank you from my heart."

He had leapt to his feet and was already shouldering his pack.

"Three o'clock on Friday," he said. "I'll not disappoint you."

Already he was swinging down the hill.

"But – look here – wait a minute . . ."

William called after him, desperately.

But the little man was already out of sight and earshot.

During the next few days William lived in a double nightmare, of which the subject was sometimes the little man arriving full of hope and pride at the Hall on Friday and being summarily dismissed by an enraged Mr Bott, and sometimes himself on whom the hand of retribution would most surely fall.

"They're going to have an entertainment," his mother said at breakfast one morning.

"What sort of entertainment?" said William hopefully.

"Zevrier, the violinist," said Mrs Brown. "He's really *famous*, you know. And *terribly* modern."

"I wonder if . . ." said William tentatively. "I mean, don't you think people would rather have a Punch and Judy show than a violinist?"

"A Punch and Judy show? Don't be so *ridiculous*, William. It's not a children's party."

By the time Friday actually arrived, however, William's natural optimism had reasserted itself. The little man had, of course, taken the whole thing as a joke and would never think of it again.

Still, as William wandered about among the guests, he kept an anxious eye upon the entrance gates.

Lord Faversham, wearing an expression of acute boredom, was being ushered by a perspiring Mrs Bott into the tent where Zevrier's recital was to take place. Then Mrs Bott went to the door to look up and down anxiously for Zevrier.

The tentful of people began to grow restive. It was quarter-past three. The audience didn't particularly want to hear Zevrier, but it had come to hear him and it wanted to get it over.

Mrs Bott, whose large face now rivalled in colour her husband's famous sauce, went into the library where her husband had sought temporary refuge with a stiff whisky and soda.

"Botty, he's not come," she said hysterically.

"Who's not come?" said Mr Bott gloomily.

"Zebra, the violin man. Oh, Botty, what shall I do? They'll all be laughing at me. Oh, Botty, isn't it *awful*!"

Mr Bott shook his head. "I can't help it," he said. "You *would* have all this set-out. I warned you it wouldn't come to no good."

"But, Botty, there they are, all waiting, an'

nothing happening! Can't you *do* something, Botty?"

"What can I do? I can't play the vi'lin . . ."

Meanwhile, outside the tent, William had turned to see a small, pack-laden figure approaching. His heart froze within him.

"Ah, my little host, I am so sorry to be late. The bus broke down. Ah, here are your guests all ready for me. I will waste no more time . . ."

Still speaking, he entered the tent, mounted the little platform that had been prepared for Zevrier, and began to set up his miniature stage.

William stood for a moment, rooted to the ground by sheer horror, then, his courage suddenly failing him, began to run down the drive and along the road that led to his home.

But just as he was rounding the corner of the boundaries of the Hall estate, he ran into the strange figure – a figure wearing an open collar, flowing tie, and shock of long, carefully waved hair. It carried a violin-case. There was no doubt at all – it was Zevrier.

William was going to hasten past, when he noticed the musician's expression – ill tempered, querulous. He remembered the appealing, rather helpless friendliness of the little Punch and Judy man. He imagined the inevitable clash between them.

Again the nightmare closed over him.

"Er – please," he began incoherently.

The musician stopped short and scowled at him. "Yes?"

"Er – are you going to the Hall?"

"Yes," snapped the musician.

"To play to them?"

"Yes."

"Are you Mr Zevrier?"

"I'm Zevrier," said the man, tossing back his hair and striking an attitude.

"Well – well – I wouldn't go to play to them if I was you."

"Why not?" snapped the musician.

William silently considered this question.

"Well, I wouldn't," he said mysteriously, "if I was you. That's all."

The musician was feeling particularly annoyed that afternoon. He was engaged in writing his autobiography, and he could not find anything interesting to put into it. He wanted it to abound in picturesque episodes, and he couldn't find even one picturesque episode to put into it.

Moreover, he disliked Mrs Bott, though he had never met her. She began all her letters to him, "Dear Mr Zebra".

"Pigs!" he burst out suddenly. "Buying immortal genius by the hour, as if it were tape at so much a yard."

"Yes," said William, "yes, that's just what I think about it."

"*You!*" said the musician, glaring at him. "How can *you* understand?"

"I *do* understand," said William fervently. "I – well, I do understand. I mean, you tell me a bit more what you feel about it. I – I mean, I want to *know* what you feel about it."

William's attitude was that every word postponed the inevitable moment of reckoning.

"You – you don't know what music is to me," said the musician striking his chest dramatically.

"Yes, I do," said William.

Experience had taught him that with a little care and skill, any argument can be prolonged almost indefinitely.

"*You* don't love music."

"Yes, I do."

"It isn't – life and breath to you."

"Yes, it is."

The musician looked at William closely. William's expression was guileless and innocent. He could not know, of course, that William was probably the most unmusical boy in the British Empire.

"Suppose," said the musician, tossing back his long hair, "suppose I played to you instead, would it be something that you'd remember all your life?"

"*Yes*," said William, fixing an idiotic smile upon his lips.

"I will," said the musician, already beginning to compose the episode – with picturesque additions – in his mind. "Let us go—"

His gaze rested on a haystack in a field next to the road. That would look well in a book of memoirs. Perhaps some artist would even be inspired to paint the scene. With an idealised boy, of course.

"Let us go there."

Arrived at the haystack, he sat down in the

shade of it, with William next to him, and drew out his violin.

He played for a quarter of an hour. Then he looked at William. William sat with a look of rapt attention on his face.

The musician could not know, of course, that in sheer boredom William had returned to his role of world potentate and was engaged in addressing his army on the eve of a great battle.

He played again, then again he looked at William.

"Another one," said William in a peremptory tone of voice that the musician took to be one of fervent appreciation.

He could not know, of course, that William was now a pirate, and was ordering his men to send yet another captured mariner along the plank.

He played again, then again looked at William. William's eyes were closed, as if in ecstasy.

He could not know, of course, that William was asleep.

He played again. The clock struck six. William sat up and heaved a sigh of relief.

"I've got to go home now," he said. "It's after my tea-time."

The musician glanced at him coldly and decided that the boy should make quite a different sort of remark in his memoirs.

They went back to the road in silence, and there parted – William to his home, and the musician to the station.

*

Mrs Bott, now on the verge of hysterics, went slowly down to the tent. To her amazement, a burst of loud laughter and clapping greeted her. She peeped in at the open flap. A Punch and Judy performance was in full and merry swing!

"I'm dreaming," she said. "Where's Zebra? Where did this thing come from?" Her eyes went to the noble lord. He was leaning forward in his seat, laughing uproariously.

After the first moment's stupefaction, everyone else had settled down to follow his example and enjoy the show. Signor Manelli was a born comedian. Toby carried his little sword with swagger.

"What's happened?" murmured Mrs Bott wildly. "I've gone potty."

But the performance was drawing to a close, amid a riot of applause. The noble lord had mounted the platform and was shaking Signor Manelli by the hand.

"Bravo!" he was saying. "I've not enjoyed anything so much for years. Not for *years*.

Now, look here, I want to book you for a party at my place in town next month. Have you a free date?"

It appeared that Signor Manelli had a free date. A fee was named, at which Signor Manelli almost fainted in sheer surprise. Suddenly the noble lord saw Mrs Bott.

"Ah!" he said genially. "Here is our hostess, to whom we owe this delightful entertainment."

Signor Manelli started forward to her eagerly. "And where is my little host?"

The mystery was suddenly clear to Mrs Bott. Botty must have engaged this man for her to fall back on, in case the Zebra person didn't turn up. It was just like Botty to do a thoughtful thing like that and not mention it.

"He's resting in the library," she said.

"I won't disturb him then," said Signor Manelli, "but give the dear little man my most grateful respects, and tell him that I shall never forget his kindness to me."

"Yes, I'll tell him," said Mrs Bott, and was at once surrounded by an eager crowd congratulating her on the success of her entertainment.

To her amazement, Mrs Bott discovered that her party had been a roaring success and that she was at last, "somebody".

When her guests had departed, she sought out her husband in the library.

"Oh Botty," she said hysterically, "how kind, how thoughtful of you to think of it. I shall never forget it – never."

He laid his hand gently on her shoulder. "You go and lie down, my dear," he said. "The excitement's gone to your head . . ."

The Browns were walking slowly homeward.

"I didn't see William there, apart from at first, did you?" said Ethel.

"He must have been there somewhere," said Mrs Brown. "I'm sure he loved the Punch and Judy show."

*

It was several months later. William sat at the table ostensibly engaged upon his homework. Mrs Brown was reading the paper and keeping up a desultory conversation with Ethel, who was embroidering a nightgown.

"It says that Punch and Judy is still all the rage in London," said Mrs Brown, "but that Signor Manelli, who started it, is taking no more engagements because he's going back to Italy. Do you remember him, dear? We saw him at that party of Mrs Bott's."

"Yes," said Ethel.

"And here's something about that Mr Zevrier, the musician that Mrs Bott once thought of having to her party, you know, before she decided to have the Punch and Judy . . ."

"What?" said Ethel absently.

"His book of memoirs has just been published. And it quotes an extract from it here. All about a musical child that he met when he was going to play at some sort of party and he stayed playing to it, and forgot the party and his fee and everything."

She looked up.

"I wonder – you know, people said that Mrs Bott had engaged him for her party, as well as the Punch and Judy show, and he didn't turn up. Could it have been *here* that he met this musical child?"

"What sort of child was it?" said Ethel.

"It quotes a description from the book," said Mrs Brown. "Here it is: 'He had deep-set, dark eyes and a pale, oval face, sensitive lips, and dark, curly hair. I saw at once that to him, as to me, music was the very breath of life.'"

Ethel laughed shortly. "No, it couldn't have been here," she said. "There isn't a child like *that* about here."

His head shielded by his hands in the attitude of one who wishes to devote himself entirely to study and shut out all disturbing influences, William grinned to himself . . .

William and the Hidden Treasure

and Other Stories

Contents

William and the Hidden Treasure

"I'm going to be a millionaire when I grow up," announced William to the Outlaws. "I'll d'vide it with you three. We'll all be millionaires."

The interest of the others became less impersonal.

Then Henry said, "William, how're we going to start gettin' the money?"

William looked at him rather coldly.

"There's a hundred ways of gettin' to be millionaires. There – there's—" then a flash of inspiration "—there's findin' hidden treasure. Why, when you think what a lot of pirates and smugglers there must have been, the earth must be *full* of hidden treasure if you know where to dig. An' if you've got a map . . ."

They scuffled joyfully homewards down the lane, playing their game in which the sole object was to push someone else into the ditch. William was neatly precipitated into it by a combined attack from Ginger and Douglas.

Then they saw William sit up and take something from the hedge.

"What is it?"

"Bird's nest."

He was frowning thoughtfully. From among the moss and feathers he had taken a small piece of crumpled paper.

He spread it out.

"*Crumbs!*" he breathed. "It's a map, of hidden treasure!"

They all tumbled down into the ditch with him. The piece of paper was crumpled but the markings on it were quite plain.

There were two circles. Under one were the

words "Copper Beech", and under the other, the word "Cedar". And between the two circles – in the centre – was a large cross. At the bottom of the paper was written "P.M. 7.10".

"It's a *map*," said William. "Look at it. All yellow and old. I expect that the pirate what made it jus' threw it into the hedge when they were takin' him off to prison, an' it's been here ever since . . . The cross is where the treasure is, of course."

"I say," said Henry. "There's a copper beech an' a cedar tree in Miss Peache's garden. He must've buried it in Miss Peache's garden."

"Right," said William. "We've got to find the 'xact spot, an' dig for it. I bet it's not as easy as it looks. He must've put some catch in it, so's if anyone who wasn't his mother or wife found the map, they wun't be able to get hold of the treasure."

"What does 'P.M. 7.10' mean?" said Ginger.

"I guess that's the catch," said William gloomily.

"There were witches in those days, you know," said Henry, "an' I bet they used to get witches to put spells on maps of hidden treasure so's only the people they meant to find 'em could find 'em."

"Yes," agreed William. "P.M. 7.10. That's the spell. It means ten minutes past seven in the evening . . . it means you'll only find it if you dig for it at ten past seven. *That's* it!"

*

They met outside the gate of Miss Peache's house a little before ten past seven that evening, armed with various implements.

Exactly between the copper beech and the cedar was a rose-bed, which would considerably facilitate digging operations. They advanced cautiously across the lawn.

But Miss Peache, prim and middle-aged, was sitting writing at a desk at a window overlooking the lawn. They returned to the road.

"We'll jus' have to wait till she's not there," said William philosophically. "It doesn't matter which day we do it, so long as it's ten minutes past seven . . ."

There followed a week of daily disappointment.

"We've gotter get her away somehow," said William. "Get her away by ten minutes past seven one day, so's we can go an' find the treasure. We'll have to find out the sort of things she's int'rested in."

"It's dreams she's int'rested in," said

Douglas. "She writes about 'em in a magazine. I know 'cause I heard my mother talking about her the other day. And she's most int'rested in people who have *real* dreams, or somethin'."

"All right," said William, "then we'd better start havin' real dreams."

The next afternoon when Miss Peache emerged from her gate as usual at two-thirty, four boys were standing there.

She could not help noticing that one of them gave a violent start of surprise, and pointed her out to the others.

"What is the matter, little boys?" she said sharply. "Is – is there anything *strange* about me?"

"Oh, no," said one of them hastily. "Oh, no. It's only that – that I *dreamed* about you last night, an' I was so surprised to see you comin' out of the gate 'cause I din' know you were a real person. I thought you were only in a dream. I'm sorry," ended the ingenuous child smugly, "if I was rude."

"Not at all. This is most interesting. Am I – er – exactly like the lady in your dream?"

"'Xactly," said the boy earnestly, "but in my dream you hadn't got a coat on. You'd got a sort of – black dress with blue in it."

"B-but how amazing! I've *got* a dress like that. I was wearing it last night. *Do* tell me – where was I in your dream? Wait a minute."

And she took out her notebook.

"You were in a sort of room," said William slowly. "There was a sort of writing-table in the window, and bookcases all round the room, and there was a sort of big blue pot umbrella-stand in a corner of the room—"

"A Nankin vase, dear," said Miss Peache, as she scribbled hard in her little notebook. "But it's all most *amazing*. One of the most *wonderful* pieces of material that's ever come my way. Now what was I *doing* in your dream?"

"You were writing at the table," said William. "An' you put your pen in a sort of big silver inkpot."

91

"Yes, that was presented to me, dear boy, by the members of a little society I was once president of. A little society for the interpretation of dreams. It has always been a great treasure to me. I could not work at all without it. If it were not in its place there on my writing-table I should not, I am quite sure, be able to carry on my wonderful work at all. Now, what did I do next, dear boy?"

But it was at this point that the Outlaws had left their point of vantage near Miss Peache's window, to go home to bed.

"I woke up," said William simply.

"Dear, dear. Never mind." She closed her notebook. "Now I want you to come to me tomorrow and tell me exactly what you dream tonight. This is all most valuable material for me. It will form the basis of my next article."

"The thing to do," said William, after she had gone, "is to take away her inkstand. Then she won't be able to write, so p'raps she'll go out . . ."

So they crept through the bushes and snatched the inkstand from the table that stood at an open window.

But even this daring step was not successful. True, Miss Peache did not write. But neither did she go out.

She sat in her study ringing up the police station every five minutes to ask if they'd had any news of her inkstand yet, and receiving messages of condolence from her friends.

William went to Miss Peache the next morning, and described a dream in which

Miss Peache busied herself continually with the telephone and wept and wrung her hands.

"Dear boy," she said, "I *really* feel that perhaps you might *dream* where my dear inkstand is. Before you go to sleep tonight, you must concentrate on where my dear inkstand is . . ."

"Where are you goin' to dream she found it?" asked Henry.

"I know!" said William. "Mr Popplestone's house. I *know* she knows him, 'cause I saw them talkin' in the road. An' I know what his study's like, 'cause once I was in it with Father . . ."

Miss Peache listened to William's dream, open-mouthed.

"It's – it's simply *amazing*. You say that in your dream you saw me going into Mr Popplestone's *study*?"

"Yes, an' it was jus' ten minutes past seven by the clock on the mantelpiece."

"And I went to the cupboard in the wall and opened it?"

"Yes."

"And I found my beloved silver inkstand in it?"

"Yes, and found your b'loved silver inkstand in it."

"And did you, in your dream, infer that he'd *taken* it?"

"Er, yes," said William. "That's how it seemed to me. It seemed to me as if he'd taken it."

"I'd have said that he was the last person in the world to do a thing like that. But, his hobby of bird study. It may be a blind to cover his secret career. However – you said that the time by the clock was ten minutes past seven?"

"Yes," said William emphatically. "Ten minutes past seven . . ."

Concealed in the bushes, the Outlaws watched Miss Peach set off from her house. Then they crept forth on the lawn.

Outside in the road was the wheelbarrow

that they had brought to take the treasure home. They carried their spades and shovels.

William also carried the silver inkstand, which was to be slipped back on to Miss Peache's study table as soon as the treasure was found.

They stood solemnly by the rose-bed, and William took out the map.

"Here it is. An' we can see the church clock so the minute it gets to ten past seven we'll start diggin' . . ."

Socrates Popplestone sat at his desk in his study. He had spent an enjoyable day watching a couple of whitethroats, and had sat down with the intention of writing up his notes.

But he wasn't writing up his notes. He was thinking about Miss Peache. In fact, lately, he'd begun to feel quite sentimental about Miss Peache.

He'd picked up a glove that she'd left in church last Sunday, and was – well, treasuring it. He roused himself to begin his bird notes.

And then – a most amazing thing happened. The door opened and Miss Peache walked in.

She said, with dramatic quietness, "Mr Popplestone, you know what I've come for. I know you took it."

A flush of guilt dyed Mr Popplestone's cheek.

His hand went to the pocket where he was carrying her glove.

"Did the verger tell you?" he asked.

He'd had a suspicion all along that the verger had seen him take it.

"No," she said, in a voice of horror. "I'd no idea that he was party to it. Why did you take it?"

"Because it belonged to you," he replied.

She stared at him in amazement.

"I've been carrying it about all day next to my heart," he went on.

"Next to your h—? Did you take the ink out of it first?"

"I never noticed any ink in it."

"You *couldn't* carry it about all day next to your heart. It's too big."

"Too big?" he said tenderly. "If it fits your hand it can't be very big."

"But I never put my whole hand into it . . . Oh, but I know where it is. A supernatural manifestation has been vouchsafed to me through a little child . . ."

She walked over to the cupboard in the wall and flung it open. In it reposed a small pile of notebooks and a bottle of cough mixture.

Miss Peache looked taken aback, but then pointed an accusing finger at Mr Popplestone, and said sternly, "Where is it?"

"Here," said the guilty man. With hanging head he brought out a crumpled white glove from his waistcoat pocket.

"W-w-w-what's that?"

"Your glove. I took it on Sunday. I thought you said you'd come for it."

"Oh. I – I – I feel rather faint, Mr Popplestone."

"Please call me Socrates," he said as he dashed wildly to the cupboard and got out the bottle of cough mixture to restore her.

"Certainly," murmured Miss Peache, "and will you call me Victoria?"

Then, first making sure that they were ready to receive her, she fainted into his arms.

The betrothed pair entered the gate of Miss Peache's house. They had agreed to be married very quietly early the next year.

"You want *looking* after, Socrates,

dearest," said Miss Peache fondly. "Oh – good gracious!"

They had turned the corner of the house, and there on the lawn were four boys engaged in digging up the rose-bed.

"Good gracious! Boys, what are you doing?"

William had seen her, and with commendable presence of mind had thrust the silver inkstand into the hole, covering it lightly with soil.

He turned to her.

"I've had another dream: I fell asleep an' I dreamed that I dug up this bed an' found your inkpot, so I came straight along to try. I b'lieve I've got to it at last. Yes. Here it is."

"How *wonderful*!" breathed Miss Peach. She turned to her fiancé.

"*There*. You doubted the boy's veracity when I told you about him. But isn't this *proof*? And such a dear boy!"

Mr Popplestone looked at William. Then he put a half-crown into William's hand – a sort of thank-offering to fate.

The next day William and Ginger slipped quietly into William's mother's drawing-room, where visitors were being entertained.

They intended to hand round the cake-stand and, with a skill born of long practice, to abstract enough cakes from it for themselves and for Douglas and Henry, who waited outside.

There was *still* lots of time to get the

treasure. They knew where it was, anyway. The map was still in William's pocket.

A woman with red hair was saying, "Peggy Marsden told me to take down the date so that I shouldn't forget her birthday – and I did, but I lost the bit of paper. Trixie says it's the seventh of October.

"I remember now. I put down P.M. 7.10 on a bit of paper to remind me. It was the bit of paper I'd begun to design Gladys and John's new garden on. I'd only just begun. I'd given them a copper beech and a cedar tree, and a sundial just between them, and then Peggy came in and I made a note of her birthday on the paper and then lost it . . ."

William and Ginger crept brokenly out of the room. Brokenly they told the other two of the ruin of their hopes.

The four of them gazed sadly into the distance, watching their millionaire life vanish into thin air.

Then William took the half-crown from his pocket.

"Well," he said, "it's enough for one ice-cream an' ginger beer for us all, anyway."

It wasn't much to salvage from the wreck of their fortunes, but it was something.

William and the Snowman

The Outlaws were sitting gloomily in the Old Barn.

"Well, at least it's trying to snow," said Ginger. "It's years since it snowed properly. In all the books you read it snows at Christmas, but it never seems to in real life."

"We had a jolly good time last holidays," said Douglas.

"We'd got Brent House last holidays," William reminded him.

The summer holidays had consisted of a glorious possession of an empty house and garden. In fact William had said that their occupation of it was a kindness to its owner.

"We can't possibly do it any harm," he had said, "an' we'll keep it aired for him with breathin' in it."

It wasn't till they heard that Brent House was sold to a Colonel Fortescue that they stood back and surveyed their handiwork.

The result was depressing: broken windows, holes in the lawn, a damaged garden seat . . .

Colonel Fortescue, when he moved in, had soon tracked down the culprits and had executed severe punishment on William.

William had sworn to avenge this deadly insult. He had even appealed to his grown-up brother, Robert, to avenge him.

But Robert flatly refused and had become deeply enamoured of the Colonel's beautiful niece, Eleanor. But the Colonel was putting every obstacle in Robert's way. The Colonel disapproved of all Eleanor's suitors – except Archie, the son of an old friend.

And Archie had come to stay at Brent House for Christmas.

So affairs stood when Ginger said, "Never mind. I bet it'll snow tonight."

And Ginger was right. They woke up the next morning to find the ground thickly covered with snow.

Moreover, Robert had lost his voice and Mrs Brown, finding that his temperature was 101°, put him to bed and sent for the doctor.

William couldn't help feeling that it was a judgement on Robert for refusing to avenge him; and so it was with a blithe spirit that William set out to spend the afternoon with the Outlaws.

After an exhilarating snowball fight they decided to make a snowman. The result was, they considered, eminently satisfactory. The snowman was life-size and well proportioned, and his features, marked out by small stones, denoted, the Outlaws considered, a striking and sinister intelligence.

"Let's pretend he's a famous criminal, an' have a trial of him," suggested William.

The others eagerly agreed.

They stood in a row and William addressed him in his best oratorical manner.

"You're had up for being a famous criminal," he said sternly, "and you'd better be jolly careful what you say."

The snowman evidently accepted the advice, and preserved a discreet silence.

Then Ginger said, "Couldn't we get a coat an' hat for him? He looks so silly like that. You can't imagine him goin' into shops an' places, an' stealin' things, all naked like that."

"Yes," said William. "Tell you what! I'll get Robert's coat an' hat. He's in bed with a sore throat, an' he won't know. I'll go'n get 'em now."

The coat was a new coat of a particularly violent tweed that Robert had bought in a desperate moment, when he felt that he must do something to cut out the wretched Archie or die. Certainly when wearing the coat he was a striking figure.

William draped it round the shoulders of the snowman. The hat tilted slightly forward at a sinister angle over the stone eyes.

"Well," he said, "I bet he looks as much like a crim'nal as anyone *could* look. Now go on, Ginger."

But, as Ginger stepped forward, William interrupted him with, "Look!"

They looked at the path that led through the field, and there was Colonel Fortescue coming along slowly, his eyes on the ground. It was obvious that he had not seen them.

"Quick!" whispered William, retreating

into the shelter of the wood. "Make snowballs for all you're worth."

He felt at last that Fate had delivered his enemy into his hands. By the time Colonel Fortescue had come abreast with them, they had a good store of ammunition.

"One, two, three – go!" whispered William.

The startled Colonel suddenly received – from nowhere, as it seemed to him – a small hail of snowballs. They fell on his eyes and ears, they filled his mouth, they trickled down his neck.

When the frenzy of the attack abated, he looked round furiously for the author of the outrage. Dusk was falling, but he plainly saw a figure in a coat and hat standing at the end of the field, near the wood. No one else was in sight.

The snowballs had come from that direction. There wasn't the slightest doubt in the Colonel's mind that the figure in the coat and hat had thrown them.

He strode across to it, trembling with rage.

The Colonel was short-sighted, but he knew that coat. It had dogged him in his walks with Archie and his niece. It clothed the form of the presumptuous Robert Brown, who dared to try to thwart his plans for his Eleanor's happiness.

"You impudent young puppy!" he said. "How dare you . . . You . . ."

Words failed him. He raised his arm and struck out with all his might.

Now a thaw had set in and Robert's tweed coat – which was very thick and warm – had completed the effect. As the Colonel struck the figure, it crumpled up, and lay, an inert mass, at his feet.

He gazed down at it through the dusk in horror; then, with a low moan, turned and fled from the scene of his crime.

The Outlaws crept out from hiding.

"Crumbs," said William. "We got him all right! Wasn't it funny when he knocked the snowman down? But, I say, I'd better be getting Robert's hat and coat back. Let's take the snowman into the wood, too, then we can pretend we never had one here if anyone makes a fuss."

They bundled up Robert's hat and coat, and rolled what was left of the snowman into the wood. Before they could make their escape, however, they saw Colonel Fortescue returning through the dusk and hastily took shelter again.

The Colonel was not alone. Archie was with him. They both looked pale and frightened.

When they reached the spot where the snowman had been, they stopped, and the Colonel looked about him.

"Great heavens!" he said. "It's gone."

"What's gone?" said Archie.

"The corpse. I left it just here."

"It couldn't have gone. You couldn't have killed him."

"I did, Archie, I swear I did. He crumpled up and fell like a log. I must have hit some vital organ. Good heavens, what shall I do? I merely meant to teach him a lesson. I didn't want to kill him."

"You're sure it was Robert Brown?"

"Absolutely. I recognised his coat even before I saw his face."

"You couldn't have killed him, sir, or his body would have been here. He may have . . ."

"Crawled into the woods to die," supplied the Colonel wildly, "or crawled home. Archie, the police may be out looking for me now. I came straight back to you, Archie, because I knew you'd stick by me through thick and thin."

But Archie seemed to have views of his own on that subject.

"That's all very well, Colonel," he said. "I'm – I'm frightfully sorry for you and all that, but – well, but you can't expect me to mix myself up in an affair of this sort."

"You mean you won't stand by me, Archie?" said the Colonel pathetically. "Think of – Eleanor!"

"Honestly, sir, I've got my reputation to think of. No man can afford to be mixed up in a case of this sort. I'm sorry, Colonel, not to be able to stay over Christmas after all, but if things are as you say, you won't be wanting visitors. You may not even be at home to entertain them."

And the gallant Archie scuttled off through the snow, to pack his things. The Colonel turned and staggered brokenly away towards the Browns' house.

William, having heard all this, ran home by

a short cut, hung up Robert's hat and coat and slipped upstairs to Robert's bedroom to see how he was. Robert was asleep, but his mother, much touched by William's brotherly solicitude, said that the doctor had left him some medicine.

"He can't talk yet, of course," she said.

William went downstairs and waited at the front gate till Colonel Fortescue arrived.

"Robert's very, very ill," volunteered William.

Colonel Fortescue gave a gasp. "He's – he's got home?" he said.

"Oh yes," said William.

"Did he – did he crawl home?"

"I don't know. I didn't see him come home."

"Have – have they had the doctor?"

"Oh yes, they've had the doctor."

"And – does he think he'll live?"

"Yes, he seems to think he'll live all right."

"Er – what has he told the doctor about – about what happened to him?"

"He can't speak yet," said William truthfully.

"He's unconscious?"

"Yes," said William. "I've jus' been up to his room an' he's quite unconscious."

"But you're sure they think he'll live?"

"Oh yes, they think he'll live."

The Colonel heaved a sigh of relief.

"I'll go home now. I'll come round again in the morning."

The Colonel arrived next morning to find William waiting by the front gate.

117

"The doctor's been, an' Robert's a lot better today," said William.

"I'm glad," said the Colonel. "And – and now they know the whole story from him, what steps are they going to take?"

"They don't know anythin' from him," said William.

"What? Hasn't he told them anything?"

"No," said William, "he's not told them anythin'."

"Oh, noble fellow!" said the Colonel. "Noble fellow!"

"The doctor says he can come out for a little walk tomorrow," said William.

"Well, my boy, if you'll let me know what time he's coming out, I'd be grateful to you. And you may play in my garden any time you like."

He walked slowly down the road, and William turned four cartwheels to celebrate the final wiping out of the insult.

Next morning Robert, on emerging from the house for his walk, well muffled and

118

wearing the famous tweed coat, was surprised to find the Colonel waiting for him.

The Colonel seized his hand and said, "Forgive me, my boy, forgive me. I – I've done you a terrible wrong."

Robert, remembering the snubs he had suffered at the Colonel's hands, quite agreed with him, but was ready to be generous.

"That's quite all right, sir," he said. "Please don't speak of it."

"I'm afraid I hurt you very much indeed," went on the Colonel.

"Well, sir, I can't say you didn't," said Robert, "but – but please don't speak of it."

"You're generous, my boy. Generous. Let me accompany you, my dear boy. Take my arm please."

Robert, rather bewildered by this sudden change of front, took the Colonel's arm, and making the most of the wholly unexpected situation, began by talking about Roman Britain – which he knew to be the Colonel's favourite subject.

The Colonel was enthralled. They reached Brent House, and the Colonel called Eleanor out to join them.

Mrs Brown, who was watching for their return, asked the Colonel and Eleanor to come in to tea.

"I'm so glad to find this boy so much better," said the Colonel.

"Yes, he's got over it very well," said Mrs Brown.

"Mrs Brown," he said, "I think that the time has come to tell you something that only Robert and I know."

Robert gaped at him. For one delirious moment he thought that the Colonel was going to publicly offer him Eleanor's hand.

"What only Robert and I know, Mrs Brown, is the cause of his recent severe illness."

"But I do know, Colonel," said Mrs Brown.

"You do?"

"Yes, his tonsils are too big. I can't think why, because neither mine nor his father's are any size at all to speak of."

"No, Mrs Brown," said the Colonel. "His tonsils are not too big. No, the truth is that on Monday afternoon, foolishly, perhaps, this young man snowballed me and, very, very foolishly, I knocked him down so violently I thought I had killed him."

He looked round the table. They were all gazing at him.

Only William was unmoved, his face wearing an expression of seraphic innocence.

"I – I – I – *snowballed* you?" gasped Robert.

"Yes, you young devil! And a jolly good shot you are, too."

"I – I – I swear I never snowballed you, sir," said Robert.

"Come, come, my boy. Better let me make a clean breast of it. You'll be denying that I knocked you down next!"

"Yes, sir," said Robert. "I certainly do."

"Good heavens!" said the Colonel. "You mean to say you've no memory of it at all? I'm afraid there must have been concussion."

But Mrs Brown assured the Colonel that Robert had been in bed on Monday afternoon.

"But, great heavens! I saw you as plainly as I see you now. Apart from everything else I knew your coat."

The Colonel turned to William.

"You said that he was unconscious."

"He was," said William innocently. "He was asleep. I thought that was what you meant."

"Well, it must have been a hallucination. A

hallucination sent me by Fate, to show me the utter worthlessness of one in whom I had trusted, and to show me the worth of one whom I had ignorantly despised."

He leant over and shook Robert warmly by the hand.

Robert grinned inanely, and then turned to meet Eleanor's eyes. They were smiling at him fondly. It was all too wonderful to be true. And yet it was jolly mysterious.

The old chap had said that he'd seen him as plainly as possible in his hat and coat. Snowballing him . . .

He looked at William.

William's face wore a shining look of innocence; his eyes were slightly upraised.

Robert knew the look well. That kid knew something about all this. He'd get hold of that kid tonight, and he'd— No, on second thoughts, Robert decided not to pursue any investigations that might alter the situation. He looked at William again.

The angelic solemnity of William's face

broke up – just for a second – then quickly restored itself . . .

The situation was highly satisfactory as it stood.

Violet Elizabeth Runs Away

"*Away from Civil'sation,*" said William scornfully.

"It's a dotty subject."

"Ole Frenchie always gives dotty subjects for essays," said Ginger.

"Ole Frenchie's against civil'sation," said Douglas. "He says he wished he'd lived in the Stone Age."

"I wish he had, too," said William.

"He says," said Henry, "that when things get too much for him he likes to leave the horrors of civil'sation behind and make for the peace an' solace of the open countryside."

"Dotty sort of thing he would say," said William.

The four Outlaws had just reached the old barn when suddenly Ginger said, "Gosh, who's this?"

It was a strange figure, dressed in a shape-less trailing coat, the face almost hidden in a thick black mop of hair.

They gazed at it in bewilderment as it approached.

"Hello, William!" said a small shrill voice.

"Gosh!" groaned William. "Violet Elizabeth Bott!"

Violet Elizabeth removed the mop-like wig.

"Yes, it's me, William," she said with her habitual lisp. "I've run away from school."

"Run away?" said William.

"Yes," said Violet Elizabeth. "I don't like it. It's a nasty place and they give you nasty food. Mince!"

Violet Elizabeth's parents had gone abroad – Mr Bott on business and Mrs Bott on a trip

to Paris – and they had parked Violet
Elizabeth at Rose Mount School, a select
boarding-school for girls on the outskirts of
the village.

"But what on earth—?" said William,
pointing to the wig that she was now dangling
in one hand.

"It's a disguise," said Violet Elizabeth
proudly. "I stole it. It's a wig. It belongs to one
of the big girls, and I stole it for my disguise,
so that I could run away. And the coat belongs

to one of the mistresses. I stole that for my disguise, too."

They stared at her helplessly.

"Yes, but what are you going to *do*?" said William.

"Stay with you," said Violet Elizabeth simply. "You must hide me so that they can't find me."

"Well, we *can't*," said William indignantly.

"But you must, William. They're nasty people at that school. I wouldn't eat mince and they said I mustn't have anything else to eat till I'd eaten it, so I shall starve to death if you send me back."

She looked at him appealingly.

"You can't send me back to starve to death, William. It would be the same as *murdering* me. And if you try to take me back, I'll *scream* an' I'll *scream* an' I'll *scream* till I'm sick, I will."

William turned to the others. "Gosh! What are we goin' to *do* with her?"

"Take her back," said Ginger.

William gave an ironic snort.

"Yes, screamin' and yellin' all down the road! That's a *jolly* good idea, I *mus'* say!"

"She bites, too," said Douglas. "She's got teeth like daggers. She bit me once an' it took *days* to get well."

"It's a sort of moral problem," said Henry.

"What d'you mean, moral problem?" said William.

"Well, she's sort of taken sanctuary with us."

"What's that?" said William. "Same as a bird sanctuary?"

"Yes, in a way," said Henry, "but it's more *serious* with humans. She's come an' asked for sanctuary an' we've got to give it to her. It would be *treachery* to hand her over to her enemies. She's – trusted us, you see. She's taken *sanctuary* with us."

"Yes, I s'pose there's somethin' in that," said William, "but we can't hide her up for the rest of our lives. An' she's fussy about food. She'd start screamin' and carryin' on."

"She's a sort of mixture of an orphan an' a refugee," said Douglas. "It makes it jolly difficult."

Violet Elizabeth had tripped over her coat and fallen at William's feet. She put the wig on again, peering up at them through the tangle of dark hair.

"It's a lovely disguise, isn't it?" she said.

"Now listen, Violet Elizabeth," said William. "You're a mixture of an orphan an' a refugee, same as Douglas says, an' we can't keep you 'cause we've nowhere to hide you, an' we can't take you home 'cause your mother's gone on a trip to Paris."

"The fairground of Europe," said Henry. "That's what I once heard someone call it."

"Yes," said Violet Elizabeth with sudden bitterness. "She's in Paris, riding on roundabouts and swinging on swings at this fairground and she doesn't care what happens to me. She just leaves me to be *poisoned* by mince an' starved to death. I won't go back to her at all now, an' it'll serve her right."

"Well, we can't go on keepin' you for the rest of our lives," said William. "It would be like that man what had to go about with an albatross tied round his neck."

Violet Elizabeth glowered at them through the forest of black hair.

"I'm not going to that nasty school," she said.

Then what could be seen of her face broke into a beaming smile.

"I *tell* you what I'll do. I'll get myself adopted. I'm sick of school an' I'm sick of my own mother. I want a nice new school and a nice new mother, so you must get me adopted."

"How could we?" said William.

"Put a notice in the post office," said Violet Elizabeth.

The Outlaws hesitated.

"Well, it's better than jus' stayin' here," whispered William to Ginger. "We'll get rid of her somehow."

They reached the post office and stood for

a minute outside, examining the notices that were displayed in the window.

They went in. It was empty except for the post mistress, who looked at them without interest.

"Well?" she said. "What can I do for you?"

"We want to put a card in the window," said Violet Elizabeth.

"Where is it?" said the post mistress.

"We haven't got one," said William. "If we tell you what we want, will you write it down?"

"What is it?" said the post mistress.

Violet Elizabeth cleared her throat impressively.

"Loveable young lady," she said, "wants to be adopted by nice person."

"All right," said the post mistress. "Now off you go, and no more of your nonsense!"

"We'll have to think of something else, then," said Violet Elizabeth when they reached the crossroads.

"Well, we can't stay here," said Douglas. "Anyone might come along an' we'd all get into a row. Look! Someone's comin' now!"

Mrs Monks and Miss Caruthers were coming down the road, deep in conversation.

"Quick!" said William, diving into the overgrown ditch. The others followed. The two women stopped at the crossroads and stood talking.

"You see," said Miss Caruthers, "this friend of mine who shall be nameless – this friend of mine wanted to find a little girl to bring up as a companion for her own little girl, who's an only child and needs companionship . . .

"Well, I got in touch with someone who seemed ideal – a widower with a little girl of the right age. I got the interview all fixed up . . . This friend of mine (who shall be nameless) is staying at the Somerton Arms in Marleigh . . .

"Anyway, I was going to take the child to the interview there this afternoon. Then I heard from the widower by this morning's post that the whole thing has fallen through.

"I've been called to the sick-bed of a dear aunt and have to rush off to the train. I tried to ring my friend up at the hotel but couldn't get through to her . . .

"I wrote a note for the gardener to take but he's not turned up. Well, there's nothing I can do about it, now. So provoking."

"I'm sorry I can't help," said Mrs Monks, "but the Women's Guild committee is waiting for me and I'm late already. Goodbye."

"Oh well," said Miss Caruthers with a sigh.

She stood irresolute for a moment. Suddenly she brightened. She had caught sight of a boy's head in the ditch.

"Boy!" she called.

Slowly, William emerged.

Miss Caruthers had not lived in the neighbourhood long enough to distinguish one boy from another. Here was a boy, she felt, who could be trusted.

"Will you do something for me, boy?" she said.

"Uh-huh," said William guardedly.

135

Miss Caruthers took a note from her handbag.

"Will you go to the Somerton Arms at Marleigh and deliver this note for me? Here's sixpence for your trouble."

William crammed the note into his pocket, and received the sixpence into a grubby palm.

"Thanks," he said, "but—"

But Miss Caruthers was already scurrying away.

The other four climbed out of the ditch.

"That's what I want to be," said Violet Elizabeth, beaming joyfully. "I want to be the little girl's companion. I'll have a nice new friend, an' a nice new mother. It's just what I want. She'll be waiting for me now and she'll never know I'm not the real one. Come on. Let's go to Marleigh quick."

They stared at her.

"Well, it's a way of gettin' rid of her," said William. "We can jus' take her there an' leave her."

He opened his hand.

"Look! She gave me sixpence."

"You must buy me a lolly then," said Violet Elizabeth, "to stop me starving to death."

"All right," said William. "If we buy you a lolly, will you promise to go back to school straight away?"

"I'll think about it," said Violet Elizabeth graciously.

Ginger ran back to the shops and returned with a lollipop.

"Now will you go back to school?" said William, handing it to her.

"No," said Violet Elizabeth, "I said I'd think about it and I've thought about it and I've decided not to."

Violet Elizabeth had dropped her lollipop on to the road, but she picked it up and proceeded to lick the dust off it.

"*Look* at her!" said Ginger. "Turns up her nose at mince an' eats dust!"

"I don't mind the taste of dust," said Violet Elizabeth. "It's quite *clean* dust. And I made up all that about the mince. I wanted to run away from school so I made all that up about the mince to give me a reason for running away. It was clever of me, wasn't it?"

"Oh, come on," said William. "Let's take her to that place an' get rid of her."

They trailed over the fields to Marleigh and the Somerton Arms.

"I'm going to have a nice new mother," said Violet Elizabeth complacently. "My own mother doesn't care for anything but riding on roundabouts in Paris, so I don't want her any more."

Mrs Bott was not riding on roundabouts in Paris. She was sitting in her bedroom at the Somerton Arms, dressed up to the nines, awaiting her visitor.

During the last few months Mrs Bott had been planning fresh manoeuvres to force her way into the ranks of the local aristocracy.

The aristocracy had been to Paris. They came back with Paris outfits and Paris hats. Mrs Bott had never been to Paris, so when Mr

Bott went to Holland on business, and decorators had taken possession of the Hall, she decided to seize the opportunity.

But her thoughts had turned more and more frequently to Violet Elizabeth at Rose Mount School. To judge from her letters, Violet Elizabeth was not happy at Rose Mount School.

Wandering through the Paris shops, Mrs Bott came to the conclusion that the root of the trouble was the fact that Violet Elizabeth was an only child. What Violet Elizabeth needed was a little companion.

She decided to move secretly. She wrote to Miss Caruthers because Miss Caruthers was a newcomer to the village who could be trusted not to spread the news.

She decided to leave Paris at once, to come home incognito, as it were, and stay quietly at the Somerton Arms till her husband had returned and the decorations at the Hall were completed.

Then she would blossom forth in all her

Paris glory. She had had things done to her face and to her hair. She had bought a Paris dress and a Paris hat.

She was wearing both hat and dress now as she sat in her bedroom in the Somerton Arms awaiting the little companion.

There was a knock at the door and the manageress of the hotel entered, closing the door behind her. She looked pale and shaken.

"There's a child," she said. "At least I think it's a child. Something about you expecting her . . ."

"Oh yes," said Mrs Bott, moving the hat sideways. "I'm expecting her. Show her in."

She opened the door and a small figure entered. The wig hid her face completely and the lollipop dangled from it, inextricably entangled in the thick black hair. The coat followed like a bedraggled tail. Mrs Bott gave an hysterical scream.

"Go away, you horrible child!" she cried. "I wouldn't let my Violet Elizabeth *see* you even. It would *kill* her. Go away!"

But, at the same moment, Violet Elizabeth had also given an hysterical scream; and heard not a word of this.

"I don't *want* you for my mother, you nasty woman! I want my own nice mother. I want my own Mummy. Go away, you nasty horrid woman! If you don't go away I'll scream and I'll scream and I'll *scream* . . ."

Mrs Bott stared at her. The voice lisping was familiar. The scream was familiar. What she could see of that small distorted face was familiar.

"Oh, my darling!" she said, throwing herself on the floor beside Violet Elizabeth.

"Go away!" screamed Violet Elizabeth again.

Mrs Bott's abrupt descent had not only displaced Violet Elizabeth's black wig, but had also displaced the Paris hat and hairdo – reducing her, almost, to her old self.

"Oh *Mummy!*" said Violet Elizabeth. "My own *nice* Mummy!"

They sat on the floor clasped in each other's arms.

And then Miss Golightly, Headmistress of Rose Mount School, entered: she had tracked her errant pupil to the Somerton Arms. Mrs Bott rose to her feet.

"Miss Golightly," she said sternly, "you have a lot to explain."

Miss Golightly explained it. The flu epidemic had reduced the staff to half its normal numbers and things had, she admitted, got a little out of hand. But that a pupil of Rose Mount School should run away was unprecedented.

She fixed a stony gaze on Violet Elizabeth.

"And *you*, Violet Elizabeth," she said, "have something to explain. Kindly explain it."

Violet Elizabeth's small sweet face wore a look of troubled innocence. "It wasn't my fault," she said plaintively. "It was those horrid boys. They made me do it."

"What boys?" said Miss Golightly.

The manageress had joined the group in the bedroom.

"There were four boys at the door . . ." she said.

But the four boys were at the door no longer. They had heard fragments of the conversation and they were following Old Frenchie's example – leaving the horrors of civilisation behind them and making for the peace and solace of the open countryside.

William Goes Shopping

"William, dear," said Mrs Brown, "I wonder if you'd do something for me this afternoon. I'll give you a shilling if you will."

William immediately assumed an expression of shining selflessness.

"It's all right, Mother," he said. "I'll help you any way I can."

"That's very sweet of you, dear," said Mrs Brown, deeply touched. "It's this," she went on. "I forgot to order the fish for dinner, and I want you to go into Hadley and get it for me. From Hallett's in the High Street. I'll write down on a piece of paper just what I want you to get."

William said, "Will you give me the shilling before I go, then I can spend it in Hadley?"

"Certainly not, dear. I shall only give you the shilling if you bring it back properly. Unless you bring it back properly I shan't give you a penny."

"S'pose," he said thoughtfully, "s'pose that I do it *nearly* all right, will you give me sixpence?"

But Mrs Brown, who had finally come to the conclusion that a penny and his bus fare would have been quite enough, answered, "Of *course* not, William. I shan't give you anything at all unless you do it *perfectly*, and a shilling's far too much in any case . . ."

It was an hour later. William was sitting on the grass near the top of the hill that led down to Hadley. He was trying for the hundredth time, without success, to make a whistle.

No need, of course, to hurry. There was only the fish to get, and he needn't be back before tea-time.

He took up his penknife again, and began to cut the hole a little wider. Perhaps that was what was wrong.

He blew – not a sound. He felt that life would hold no more savour for him if he couldn't find out how to make whistles.

Suddenly he heard a voice behind him.

"An' what are ye trying to do, young sir?"

He turned around.

An old man sat on a chair outside a cottage door. So intent had William been upon his whistle that he had not noticed him before.

"Make a whistle," he said and returned to his attempts.

"It's the wrong way," quavered the old man. "Ye'll never make a whistle that way."

William wheeled round. "D'you know how to make a whistle?"

"Aye. 'Course I do," said the old man. "I were the best hand at makin' a whistle for miles when I were your age. Let's look at it now . . ."

He inspected William's abortive efforts at whistle-making with unconcealed contempt.

"Ye'll never make a whistle this way. Never. Where's your sense, boy?"

"I dunno. I – I sort of thought that was how you did it."

"Tch! Tch!" said the old man. "What on earth are boys coming to? I'd've bin ashamed at your age! I would for sure."

"Could you show me how to do it?"

"How can I! Now you've cut it about like this? You'll have to get me another reed. Quickly."

"I don't know where there are any," said William.

"Tch! Tch! I don't know what boys are coming to. Through that stile, across the field. You'll find them growing by the river. Why, when I was a boy—"

But William had already vaulted the stile. He returned panting a few minutes later with an armful of reeds.

The old man was waiting for him with his penknife. William handed him a reed, and he began to cut it at once.

"This way . . . an' then that . . . don' make the hole too big . . . I wish I'd got my ole dad's penknife. An' I *ought* to have it by rights too."

"Now, Dad," said a woman's voice from inside the cottage. "Don't start on that again."

"All very well sayin' don' start on that again," said the old man. "I *ought* to have my ole dad's penknife by rights. He'd promised it to me. Charlie always wanted it too, but my ole dad he promised it to me, an' left it to me in his will."

A middle-aged woman came to the cottage door.

"Yes, he left it to you in his will, and you lost it."

"I did *not* lose it," said the old man, beginning to shape another whistle. "I lent it to Charlie an' he never give it me back."

"He says he did an' you lost it."

"No," said the old man. "Others have seen it up there, behind his shop. He keeps it on his desk. Makes a joke of it to 'em. He says I can have it if I'll come for it. If I'd got the use of my legs . . . I tell you, that penknife—"

"I'm sick to death of hearing about the penknife," said the woman, and went back into the cottage, slamming the door.

The old man went on talking and whittling.

"You don' find any knives like my old dad's now. A great big one of horn, with his 'nitials on. Charlie borrers it an' never gives it me back. Always like that, he was. From a boy. Cunnin' . . . If I'd got the use of me legs, he wouldn't have dared. I'd've gone down to his shop an' had it off him. Now have a blow at that an' see if it's all right."

William had a blow. It certainly was all right.

"Now you make one all yourself," he said to William.

He watched eagerly, as if the fate of both of them depended upon the result. When finally William, almost trembling with suspense, raised the whistle to his lips and blew a shrill blast, he clapped his gnarled hands and chuckled again.

"Fine!" he said. "Fine! Now, that's a proper whistle, that is. Shameful – warn't it? – to think of a boy of your age not being able to make a whistle. Hundreds of them I've made, with my old dad's knife when I was a boy. Oh, when I think of that Charlie havin' it – well—"

"Where does he live?" asked William.

"Got a little tobacconist's in the High Street next to the boys' outfitters. Well, now you can make a whistle, can't you?"

"Yes," said William, and blew another piercing blast.

He walked up the road to the High Street as light-heartedly as if he trod air. He could make whistles. He saw himself in the future, making hundreds and hundreds of whistles. He'd teach Ginger and Douglas and Henry. They'd all make whistles . . .

And his heart overflowed with gratitude to his benefactor . . . His old dad's penknife . . .

William began to examine the shops he passed. A tobacconist's, yes, and next door to it a boys' outfitters. William stood still. No one was passing. He peered into the tobacconist's shop. It was empty. He tiptoed in. But no one appeared.

Summoning all his courage, he tiptoed to the doorway of the inner room. It was empty. In the corner by the window was an old-fashioned desk, and on it was an enormous ancient horn penknife.

William's eyes gleamed. He darted forward, seized it, then turned to run back to the road. But then he heard an angry shout behind him, and knew that someone had come running down a small flight of stairs.

He leapt through the shop to the street. The door of the boys' outfitters next door was open. William plunged into it. A bald-headed man was fast asleep in a chair behind the counter. He stirred. He was obviously about to open his eyes.

William looked about him desperately. He pulled aside a curtain and leapt into the shop window where stood a row of wax models about his own size wearing tweed shirts.

He snatched a label: "Latest Fashion 63s." from the nearest, pinned it on to his own suit, and took his place at the end of the row.

Immediately afterwards, just as the bald-headed man was opening his eyes, a short stout man plunged through the doorway.

The bald-headed man looked at him sternly.

"What on earth's the matter?" he said indignantly. "Anyone would think the place was on fire."

"A boy," panted the stout man. "In my back room . . . chased him out . . . came in here . . ."

The bald-headed man looked about him. "Nonsense!" he said. "No boy's been in here."

"I saw him. I tell you, I *saw* him."

"Very well. Find him, then. I've seen no boys."

The stout man went into the inner room, and then came out again.

"No," he said. "He doesn't seem to be any-where here."

"He probably went next door," said the outfitter. "I don't believe there ever was a boy."

But Charlie had already gone next door.

William, standing to attention among the row of models, holding his breath, was beginning to feel more and more ill at ease. The bald-headed man was fully awake now, and sat barring his only way of escape. At any time he might be discovered.

He had taken advantage of the fluster of Charlie's entry, to seize a large straw hat from the floor near him and put it on his head, dragging it down over his eyes.

William scanned the passers-by fearfully from beneath the brim, standing very still, trying not to breathe. One woman, who held a little girl by the hand, stopped and looked at the models attentively. William could hear their comments.

"Well," she said, "I don't think much of the suit the end one's got on, do you, Ermyntrude?"

"Naw," said the little girl.

"It's not a suit *I'd* like to pay sixty-three shillings for."

"Naw," said Ermyntrude. "And its 'at's too big."

"Not what they used to be – none of these shops."

Ermyntrude was bending down in order to see under the large brim. "It's gotta nugly face too."

"Well, they can't 'elp their faces," said the woman. "They make 'em with wax out of a sort of mould, and when the mould gets old the faces begin to come out odd. An' sometimes they get a bit pushed out of shape."

"This one's mould was old," said Ermyntrude, "an' pushed out of shape, too, I should think."

"Yes. Come on, love. We'll never get the shoppin' done at this rate."

They passed on. William was heaving a sigh of relief when he saw that half a dozen small boys were flattening their noses against the glass.

"They're dead boys," one of them was saying in low fearful tones. "I know they're dead boys. My brother told me. The shopman goes out after dark catchin' 'em.

"Then when he's killed 'em he dresses 'em up and puts 'em in his shop window. If you was to come past his shop after dark he'd get you.

"My brother said so. My brother once met him after dark carryin' a sack over his shoulder . . ."

They gazed with awe and horror. Suddenly the smallest boy gave a scream of excitement.

"*Oo!* Look! Look at the one at the end, the one with the hat. He forgot to put new clothes on that one. It's got its old ones on."

They contemplated William in tense silence.

Then the smallest one said, "It's *breathin'*. Watch it! It's *breathin'*! It's not dead."

They gazed at this phenomenon, open-mouthed. William, though trying to retain immobility, found the spectacle of their noses flattened to whiteness against the glass irresistibly fascinating.

"Look!" said the smallest one again, craning his head to look under the hat. "It's movin' its eyes too. I can see it movin' its eyes. It's comin' alive! It's comin' alive! They do sometimes. Moths do sometimes after you've put 'em in a killin' bottle."

"Go an' tell him it's comin' alive," said another.

"*You* go'n tell 'im."

At this moment the hat slid forward. Instinctively, William caught it and replaced it on his head.

Seeing that the situation was completely lost, he relieved his feelings by pulling his most hideous face at the row of gaping spectators, and then put out his tongue.

"*Oo!* G'n, tell him quick. It's coming alive. It'll get away in a minute."

The smallest boy put his head into the shop, and called out, "I say, mister! One of them boys in the window's comin' alive—"

With a roar of fury the proprietor rushed after them. They fled before him down the street. Seizing his opportunity, William leapt from the window, out of the shop and sped along the road and up the hill.

The old man still sat outside his cottage door. William flung him the penknife as he passed. The old man's voice followed him on his headlong flight.

"Me old dad's penknife! Glory be! Me old dad's penknife!"

The bus was waiting at the top of the hill, and William leapt upon it, just as it started off.

A quarter of an hour later, he was walking jauntily homewards. He'd had a jolly exciting afternoon, and he'd learnt how to make whistles.

He put his hand in his pocket and encountered a mysterious envelope with something hard inside. He took it out and opened it. Money. Money? What on earth—?

And then suddenly he remembered. Hallett's. The fish. The errand he'd gone into town for. He'd forgotten all about it.

The shilling. He'd been going to have a shilling for it. It was too late to go back now. He entered the house slowly with a sinking heart. His mother came out of the drawing-room.

"Oh, William darling, I'm *so* sorry. I *quite* forgot that Hallet's was closed this afternoon," she said. "I remembered as soon as you'd gone."

William tried to assume the expression of one who had gone on an errand to a shop and found it closed.

"Did you feel very cross with me, darling?" went on his mother.

"No," said William. "No, not at all, Mother."

"Well, we're going to have omelettes instead of fish, dear, so it's all right. And you've brought the money back?"

He handed her the money.

"You can have the shilling, of course, dear, just as if you'd done it, because it was only the accident of the shop being closed that prevented you. *And* another sixpence because it must have been so annoying for you."

William swaggered down the road, his whistle at his lips, emitting blasts with every breath. One hand was in his pocket, lovingly fingering his shilling and his sixpence.

First he'd go to Mr Moss's sweet shop and buy some bull's eyes, big 'uns. Then he'd meet the other Outlaws and teach them how to make whistles.

Life seemed to stretch before him – one glorious opportunity for whistle-making.

He gathered breath and blew a piercing blast – a paean of exultation and triumph and joy of life.

William's Wonderful Plan

and Other Stories

Contents

William's Wonderful Plan

William noticed the caravan the first morning it appeared and formed his plans at once for acquaintance with its owners.

Caravans had a peculiar fascination for William. He had always found in caravan-dwellers, whether of gypsy or bohemian persuasion, a pleasing freedom from the conventions and prejudices of regular house-holders.

Immediately after school he made his way down to the caravan and hung about it. He could see a man in the next field seated at an easel, painting.

William was just about to draw closer to the caravan when a little girl appeared suddenly in the doorway. She was about William's age with a round, dimpled face and dark curls.

"What are you doing there, boy?" said the little girl in a clear voice. "Come and help me wash up."

Impressed despite himself by the imperiousness of the little girl's voice, William managed to preserve his manly independence so far as to reply, with a swaggering laugh, "Huh, you needn't try bossing me, 'cause I'm jolly well not goin' to be bossed by any ole girl."

But, even as he said it, he was turning to make his way meekly to the caravan, and within a few minutes was engaged in washing up and sweeping out the tiny room under the little girl's orders.

She informed him, while he did so, that she had had measles, and that this caravan holiday with her father was her final convalescence, before she returned to school.

"My father," she informed him, "is the greatest artist in the world. He can cook, too, but he's very untidy."

And she bustled about, dusting, tidying, putting away the tea things.

She was certainly not William's ideal caravan-dweller. On the other hand, her dimples were distinctly attractive, and William found her imperious manner intriguing.

After that, he called there regularly. He had become the little girl's willing slave. The artist addressed him vaguely as "boy" whenever he met him, and seemed to feel no curiosity about him.

William had told no one about the caravan and its occupants, but he soon found that the news had spread through the village.

Mrs Bott, of the Hall, coming to invite William to a children's garden party, added, "And I'm going to ask that little girl who's camping here with her father. He's quite distinguished, I hear. An RA and all that . . ."

When Mrs Bott had gone, William, who hated visits to the Hall, did his best to extricate himself from the festivity.

"I'm sure I shan't be well enough," he pleaded to his mother. "It's no good me goin' there with an illness comin' on, an' givin' it to everyone there."

"But you haven't got an illness, William," protested his mother.

"I din' say I'd got one jus' this minute. I only said I felt I was goin' to have one that afternoon. I mean it doesn't seem fair to people to say you'll go to a place when you *know* you're only goin' to give them all an illness."

"If you think you're going to be ill, William, I'll ask the doctor to call."

William beat a hasty retreat.

To his surprise, the little girl actually wanted to go to the party.

"Don't be silly, William," she said. "Of *course* I want to go. It's a *party*. The only thing is . . ."

She sighed and the sparkle died away from her face.

"Yes?" said William.

"I haven't got a proper party dress . . . I've just got an old muslin one, all washed out and ever so much too short . . . and all the others will have lovely dresses. I shan't enjoy it a bit . . ."

"Well, don't go then," said William.

She stamped her small foot. "Don't be *silly*. I tell you I *want* to go."

"Well, ask your father to get you a new dress."

"No, I won't. He's poor and he's working hard and he mustn't be worried. You see, the one I have does all right for school but it'll look *awful* at a garden party, because I *know* all the others will have nicer ones."

"Now, look here," said William impulsively, "don't you worry. I'll see that you have a nice party dress for it."

He was aghast when he heard himself make this astounding offer, but it was too late to retract. Her face beamed with joy.

"Oh, William! Will you *really*?"

He found her gratitude very pleasing.

"'Course I will," he said, with a short laugh. "A little thing like that's nothin' to me. Nothin' at all."

"But William, you mustn't let anyone know you're getting it for me, will you? I should feel like a beggar if you did."

William gave another short laugh.

"Oh, no," he said. "'Course I wouldn't do that. Oh no. I'll get you a jolly nice new party dress, a jolly nice new one. You needn't worry about *that*."

The little girl beamed once more.

"Oh, William!" she said. "You are wonderful."

"Mother," he said thoughtfully that evening. "I don't mind goin' to this party of Mrs Bott's, if I can go in fancy dress."

"But of *course* you can't go in fancy dress, William," said his mother firmly. "It isn't a fancy dress party."

"P'raps it is, and she forgot to say. Anyway, I think I ought to have a fancy dress ready, case it is."

"But William, what *nonsense*! And even if it is, you've got your Red Indian suit."

"I'm sick of that ole Red Indian suit. I want to go as a little girl. I want you to buy me a little girl's party dress, so that if we find it's fancy dress at the last minute, I can go in it."

"William, I can't think what's come over you."

"Nothin's come over me. Surely I can go to a fancy dress party as a little girl if I want to."

"But there is no fancy dress party," protested Mrs Brown again.

"Well, will you give me a little girl's party dress and count it my Christmas present?"

"No, William, no, and I've no time to stay here talking nonsense with you like this. I've got the lunch to see to."

William decided to approach the six-year-old Violet Elizabeth Bott in whose honour the garden party was being held.

He thought of the endless succession of elaborate frocks in which her small person made its appearance at all the local functions.

She was, of course, much smaller than the little girl of the caravan, but surely, thought William, the little girl could make one dress for herself out of two of Violet Elizabeth's.

He approached the Hall cautiously and found Violet Elizabeth sitting on an upturned wheelbarrow.

"I'm a princess, William," she announced with her habitual lisp. "An' you're my subject. You've got to bow when you speak to me."

Ordinarily, William would have ignored her, but to the lady's gratification and secret surprise he bowed.

"Look here," he began, "I want to ask you something."

"You must say 'Your Royal Highness' when you speak to me," said Violet Elizabeth imperiously.

"Your Royal Highness," muttered William. "Look here . . . I want to ask you—"

Violet Elizabeth had leapt from the wheel-barrow.

"I want to go for a ride," she said. "Make my throne into a chariot."

William obediently turned over the wheel-barrow.

"Now, look here," he said. "What I want to ask you—"

"Now you're my coachman," said Violet Elizabeth, reposing on the wheelbarrow and arranging her miniature skirt about her with dignity. "Give me a ride, coachman."

Still forcing his proud spirit to this uncon-genial servitude, William took up the handles of the wheelbarrow, and began to push the small tyrant round the lawn.

"Now, look here," he began again rather breathlessly. "This is what I wanted to ask you—"

"You must say 'Your Royal Highness' when you speak to me," said Violet Elizabeth. "If you don't, I'll have your head chopped off for treason. And go faster!"

"Your Royal Highness," said William. "Now this is what I wanted to ask you—"

"I'm having a new frock from London for our party," announced Violet Elizabeth.

It was a heaven-sent opening.

"I say," panted William, "you've got lots of party frocks, haven't you?"

"Hundreds an' hundreds, an' say 'Your Royal Highness' or I'll have you arrested for treason."

"Your Royal Highness – well now, suppose there was another little girl—"

Violet Elizabeth's interest was suddenly aroused.

"Yes. Go on."

"Suppose there was another little girl that was invited to your party, but had only got a very old frock to come in, wouldn't you want to give her some of your old party frocks so that she can have a nice one to come in?"

A seraphic smile appeared upon Violet Elizabeth's angel countenance.

"No, I wouldn't," she said. "I'd *like* her to come in an old frock, 'cause it would make my new frock seem smarter than ever."

There was only one thing to do and William did it. He tipped the young autocrat urgently out of the wheelbarrow on the lawn, then set off himself quickly down the drive.

For a second, fury and amazement deprived Violet Elizabeth of the power of speech. Then it returned and scream after shrill scream rent the peaceful summer morning.

William was slowly approaching the caravan. He had almost decided to admit failure, but when the little girl came running across the field to him he could not find it in his heart to disappoint her.

"Oh, William," she cried excitedly. "Have you got it?"

"Er – not yet," said William, trying rather unsuccessfully to assume an airy manner. "There's plenty of time."

"You have got a plan, haven't you, William?" she said, anxiously.

He laughed a carefree laugh that rang slightly hollow.

"'Course I have," he said. "I should jolly well think I've got a plan all right."

They reached the caravan, and he followed her into it. A much-washed white muslin dress lay over a chair. The little girl held it up.

"It looks *awful*," she said sorrowfully. "I'd rather go in it than not go at all, of course, but

I shall feel dreadful if I have to wear it. It's all washed to bits and it's miles too small. But – you *have* promised to get me a new one, haven't you, William?"

"Oh yes," said William with a ghastly smile. "Oh yes, don't you worry about that."

The church clock struck five. She flung the dress over the chair again.

"That's tea-time. I'd better go and fetch Father. Be an angel, William, and put on the kettle. The water's in the petrol tin, you know."

She ran off across the field and William, heavy-hearted, lit the spirit-lamp as he had seen the little girl do, and filled the kettle from the petrol tin.

He had often seen the little girl fill the kettle from the petrol tin, but he had never realised that the caravan contained two petrol tins, one full of water, the other of paraffin, and it was from the paraffin tin that William had filled the kettle.

The next few moments were like the climax

of a nightmare. As he placed the kettle on the spirit stand a sheet of flame burst out, precipitating him through the caravan door and on to the grass outside.

Through a whirligig of stars, he saw two men who happened to be passing leap into the caravan and fling their coats upon the bright sheet of flame.

The flame died down. Through eddies of smoke William, sitting with a blackened face and singed hair upon the grass, saw the scorched remnants of the little girl's dress, now about the size of a pocket handkerchief, still reposing on the chair.

He gazed at it for a few moments, sprang to his feet, and fled from the scene of ruin.

For the next few days he felt as if he were still living in a nightmare. He dare not revisit the little girl; his brain seemed to be numbed and stupefied by the immensity of the catastrophe.

The day of the garden party arrived. He could think of nothing but the little girl, deprived by his act of the party to which she had been looking forward.

She had said that she would rather go in the old muslin dress than not go at all. And he had burnt the old muslin dress.

He walked slowly and in a hangdog fashion towards the Hall. The little girl would not be at the party, of course, but suppose she were waiting outside to reproach him . . .

He entered the gate, and crossed over the lawn to a group of little boys and gaily dressed little girls.

Suddenly he heard a cry of "William", and to his amazement he saw the little girl detach herself from the group and come across the lawn to him. She wore a very pretty and obviously new dress of pale pink.

"Oh, *William*," she was saying, "you are *wonderful*! Oh, William, thank you so much. It was so clever of you, and I'm so sorry that I didn't really believe you'd got a plan. And it was such a *wonderful* plan."

William was gazing at her, open-mouthed.

"W-w-w-w-what?" he demanded.

"Why, to burn my old dress so that the insurance people should give me a new one. They've given me a lovely new one, haven't they? Oh, William, it was so clever of you to think of it."

William recovered himself quickly. He assumed his easy swagger, smiling at her in affectionate condescension.

"Oh, that's all right," he said. "A little thing like that's nothin' to me."

Parrots for Ethel

"Now," said William to Douglas and Ginger, "'bout this animal lecture what I'm going to give. We'll have it in our summer-house, an' I'll lecture on 'em. An' we'll have all our cats and Jumble. And we'll colleck some more insecks, an' we'll have Ginger's dormouse."

"Right," said Ginger, "let's go and fetch the dormouse."

They passed the drawing-room where Ethel sat with George and Hector. George was Douglas's elder brother; Hector was Ginger's. Both young men were infatuated with Ethel.

"Douglas drove me half-mad with a beastly

mouth organ yesterday," groaned George, "till I took it from him and chucked it into the pond."

"Same here with Ginger's trumpet," said Hector.

"Well I'm sure no boy ever was half as bad as William," said Ethel with a sigh. "He broke a vase that was one of my greatest treasures yesterday with his bow and arrow. I confiscated them of course."

Both Hector and George made an inarticulate murmur of deep sympathy.

"And William had a thing," said Ethel dreamily, "that was supposed to sound like a bird chirping. Only it didn't. It went through and *through* my head."

"Oh what a *shame*," said Hector and George simultaneously, in passionate indignation.

"I'm very fond of birds," continued Ethel.

"What sort do you like best?"

"I think that parrots are rather sweet," said Ethel. "Don't you?"

Neither spoke.

"I remember once," went on Ethel, "a friend of mine had to go into quarantine for measles, or something like that, and a friend of hers gave her a parrot to be comforting for her. He gave it in rather a nice way, too. He put it on the garden seat on the lawn, and sent in a letter to say that if she'd look out of her window she would see a little friend who had come to keep her company. Or something like that. She was always devoted to that parrot."

It was the next morning. Ethel was staring wildly at a letter she held in her hand.

"Daphne's got measles, and I was with her last night. Oh, what shall I do?"

"You'll have to go into quarantine, I'm afraid, dear," said her mother placidly.

William received the news without emotion. A more terrible tragedy had happened than Ethel's quarantine. Ginger's dormouse had died in the night.

Ginger and Douglas took the dead body to the summer-house, leaving William alone on the lawn, gloomily considering the prospect of his lecture thus deprived of its star turn.

He didn't at first see Ginger's brother Hector who had come round to the side of the house looking pale and distraught.

"This is terrible news," began Hector.

"Yes, isn't it?" said William. "Terrible."

"She seemed all right yesterday," continued Hector.

"She was, she was quite all right yesterday.

190

I think it was eatin' those berries."

"What berries?"

"Those berries Ginger gave her."

"Wha—? Did Ginger give her some berries?"

"Oh yes, all sorts of different coloured kinds of berries what he found about the garden and she ate them all."

"But I heard in the village it was measles."

"No, it's worse than measles. She's dead. She died in the night."

"*What?*"

"She's dead. When Ginger 'n' me came to clean out her cage this morning we found her dead."

"Clean out her c—? What the dickens are you talking about?"

"Our mouse," said William. "Weren't you?"

The visitor controlled himself with an effort.

"No. I was talking about your sister, Ethel."

"Oh, Ethel. Oh no. No, it's not measles, it's somethin' else. Quarantine or somethin'."

Hector turned on his heel and strode away. He'd remembered suddenly what Ethel had said. He'd get her a parrot.

William remained upon the garden bench, plunged in gloom. The voice of George broke upon his meditations.

"Well, I'm very sorry to hear this," began George.

William's heart warmed to him. Here, at any rate, was sympathy.

"Yes," he said. "Yes, it was an awful shock to us all to find her dead this mornin'."

"*What?*"

Explanation followed, and George walked quickly down the road. He'd suddenly remembered what Ethel had said about the parrot yesterday. He'd get her one.

William rejoined the others in the summer-house.

"Tell you what. We'll put up a notice asking people to lend us an'mals, or give us an'mals, like what they do to the zoo."

Ten minutes later they gathered round to look at William's notice. It read as follows:

"mister william brown is going to leckcher on anmals and will be gratful to anyone who will give or lend him anmals to be leckchered on mister william brown is out now lookin for valubul insex, but will be back before dinner mister william brown will be glad if people givin him anmals to be leckchered on will put them on the seat in the back garden an tie them up if they are savvidge anmals mister william brown's vallubul assistunts are ginger and douglas."

They pinned the notice on the side gate and sallied forth in search of insects.

A short time before their return, Hector appeared looking very hot and breathless. He held a parrot in a cage.

He had cycled frenziedly into the nearest town and had spent practically his last penny on it. He found a garden seat conveniently situated.

He then slipped a letter quietly through the letter box. In the letter he said that if she would look out of the window, she would see upon the garden seat a little friend who had come to keep her company.

Then, smiling fatuously to himself, he tiptoed away.

Hardly had he disappeared, when the Outlaws returned. They had found only one species of caterpillar.

They turned the corner of the house, and there upon the garden seat was a parrot in a cage. They rushed to it and bore it off in triumph to the summer-house.

The parrot uttered a shrill scream of laughter, and said with deep feeling, "Go away, I hate you."

"Wonder what they eat?" said Ginger.

"I say, where's that tin with my caterpillar in?" said William. "Who's took it?"

"You left it on the garden seat, when we fetched the parrot in," said Douglas.

They hurried out to the garden seat.

It was empty.

Meanwhile, a housemaid had found Hector's note on the mat and taken it up to Ethel's room. Ethel's room did not happen to overlook the garden. She read the note with a smile, almost as fatuous as Hector's.

"A little friend to keep you company." Oh, it was very, very sweet of him. She opened the door, and called to the housemaid.

"Emma, will you bring me something that you'll find upon the garden seat."

Emma went out and returned with a small

tin. Inside were several leaves and a big furry caterpillar.

"Oh, *that's* his idea of being funny, is it?" said Ethel viciously. "Well, it's not *mine.*"

And she flung the tin furiously into the fire-place.

At that very moment, the faithful George was tiptoeing softly round the side of the house, bearing a parrot in a cage, and the Outlaws were returning from another cater-pillar expedition.

"Funny we only caught one of those caterpillars again," said William.

"Well, one's enough to lecture on, I suppose," said Douglas.

William had stopped suddenly, and was staring in blank amazement.

"There – there's another parrot on the seat. Look. It is, isn't it? It *is* another parrot, isn't it?"

"Yes," said Ginger, "it cert'nly is. Seems sort of funny they should *all* be givin' us parrots, don't it?"

They took it into the summer-house, and the other parrot greeted it with a sardonic laugh. The latecomer gazed round with a supercilious air, and finally screamed, "Great Scott."

Then William said, "Where's that tin with the caterpillar in?"

"You left it on the bench again, William," said Douglas.

They went out and stood around the empty bench.

"*Well*," said William, "it's mos' *mysterious*. Someone's pinched this one too."

Upstairs Ethel was hurling the second caterpillar and tin furiously into the fireplace.

It was late afternoon. Hector, still wearing his fatuous smile, came round the corner of the house. He felt that he couldn't wait a minute longer without hearing an account of Ethel's rapturous glee on the receipt of his present.

A housemaid opened the door.

"I just called to see if the parrot was settling down all right," said Hector.

"The parrot?"

"Yes. The parrot that arrived this morning."

"No parrot arrived this morning, sir."

"W-what? Are you sure?"

"Oh quite sure, sir. There's no parrot in the house at all."

"Not – er – not in Miss Brown's room?"

"Oh no, sir. I've just been there."

Dazedly, Hector walked away. Then he

stopped. There, just outside the closed door of the summer-house, stood William with a parrot in a cage.

The two parrots had begun to hold a screaming contest, till William was forced to take George's outside.

Hector's first impulse was to hurl himself upon William and accuse him of stealing his parrot, but on approaching nearer he saw that it was not his parrot, and it was not his cage.

"Whose is that parrot, William?" he asked pleasantly.

"Mine," said William.

"W-where did you get it?" said Hector still more pleasantly.

"Someone gave it to me."

There was a short silence.

Then Hector said, "I'm – I'm willing to buy that parrot from you, William."

A sudden gleam had come into William's eye.

"I tell you what I'll do. I'll swap it with you."

"What for?" said Hector hopefully.

"I want to give Ginger a present. One of those nice trumpets. You can get them at Foley's in the village. They cost six shillings. I'll swap it with you for one of those trumpets to give to Ginger."

For a minute there was murder in Hector's eye, then he gulped and said, "Very well. You wait here."

Soon he was back with the trumpet. He hurled it at William, seized the parrot cage and disappeared. He was going to write a beautiful little note, fasten it to the cage, and deliver it in person at the front door.

Inside the summer-house the Outlaws were dancing a dance of exultation around Ginger, who was producing loud but discordant strains from his magnificent new trumpet.

This festive gathering was, however, broken by the sudden advent of George. Like Hector, he'd been informed that no parrot had entered the house that day.

He then caught a glimpse of the Outlaws in

the summer-house, leaping wildly about a parrot in a cage.

"You little *thieves*," he panted. "What do you *mean* by taking my parrot?"

"'S not your parrot, 's ours."

George looked at the parrot. William was right. It wasn't his cage. He gulped. He began to make tentative enquiries as to the exact value William set upon his parrot.

It appeared that William was willing to exchange it for a mouth organ, one of the six shilling ones from Foley's, because he wanted to give one to Douglas as a present.

George went off furiously to buy the mouth organ, returned with it, flung it at the Outlaws and stalked off with his parrot.

At a discreet distance, the Outlaws followed George round and out of the side gate. George was going to take the parrot in at the front door, ring the bell, and deliver it in person.

And then, to his amazement, he saw Hector blithely approaching from the opposite direction, also carrying a parrot in a cage.

They met at the gate. Each recognised his own parrot and cage in the hand of the other.

Simultaneously they shouted, "So *you* stole my parrot!"

The Outlaws watched in mystified delight. A shabby-looking man who happened to be passing also stopped to form an interested audience.

George turned round, thrust the cage into William's arms with a curt, "Take that", and began to roll up his sleeves.

Hector turned to the shabby-looking man, thrust his cage into his arms, and the next minute, George and Hector were giving a splendid boxing display upon the high road with bare fists.

The shabby man crept softly away with his parrot and cage. Very thoughtfully, William carried his cage up to Ethel's room.

"Erm, I won't come in, Ethel," he said, "'cause of catching your quarantine illness, but I've brought you a little present. I heard you said you'd like a parrot, and I brought you one."

Ethel was deeply touched. "How very kind of you, William," she said. "I – er – you can have your bow and arrow back. I'm sorry I took it from you. It's very kind of you to bring me the parrot."

Willliam received his bow and arrow with perfunctory thanks. Just at that moment the housemaid came up with a note. Ethel tore it open.

"Why, it's all right," she said. "Daphne hasn't got measles after all. The rash has all gone. And the doctor said she's not got it at all. And they want me to go to tea. And they've got that handsome artist coming. Oh, how jolly. I'll start at once."

A few minutes later, Ethel, accompanied by William, Ginger and Douglas, set out from the front door. At the gate Hector and George came forward to greet them.

The fight was just over, abandoned by mutual consent. Ethel passed them head in air. They stood, gaping after her in helpless bewilderment.

The Outlaws turned back to look at them. Ginger and Douglas raised trumpet and mouth organ to their lips and uttered defiant strains. William waved his bow and arrow in careless greeting.

They had had a most successful day. There had been, it's true, certain mysterious elements in it that they couldn't understand, but that didn't matter. They were perfectly happy.

The Bishop's Handkerchief

Until now William had taken no interest in his handkerchiefs as accessories. But last week, Ginger (a member of the circle known to themselves as the Outlaws, of which William was the leader) had received a handkerchief as a birthday present from an aunt in London.

William, on hearing the news, had jeered, but the sight of the handkerchief had silenced him. It was a large handkerchief, larger than William had conceived it possible for handkerchiefs to be. It was made of silk, and contained all the colours of the rainbow.

Round the edge, green dragons sported upon a red ground.

Ginger displayed it, fully prepared for scorn and merriment, but there was something about the handkerchief that impressed them all . . .

The next morning Henry appeared with a handkerchief almost exactly like it, and the day after that Douglas had one. William felt his prestige lowered. He – the born leader – was the only one of the select circle who did not possess a coloured silk handkerchief.

That evening he approached his mother.

"I don't think white ones is much use," he said.

"Don't scrape your feet on the carpet, William," said his mother placidly. "I thought white ones were the only tame kind – not that I think your father will let you have any more. You know what he said when they got all over the floor and bit his finger."

"I'm not talkin' about *rats*," said William. "I'm talkin' about handkerchiefs."

"Oh – handkerchiefs! White ones are far the best. There's nothing better than white linen."

"Pers'nally," said William with a judicial air, "I think silk's better than linen, an' white's so tirin' to look at. I think a kind of colour's better for your eyes. My eyes do ache a bit sometimes. I think it's prob'ly with keep lookin' at white handkerchiefs."

"Don't be silly, William. I'm not going to

buy you silk handkerchiefs to get covered with mud and ink and coal, as yours do . . ."

William decided to investigate Robert's bedroom. He opened Robert's dressing-table drawer and turned over the handkerchiefs.

He caught his breath with surprise and pleasure. There, beneath all Robert's other handkerchiefs, was a larger, silkier, more multi-coloured handkerchief than Ginger's or Douglas's or Henry's.

He gazed at it in ecstatic joy. He slipped it into his pocket and, standing before the looking glass, took it out with a flourish, shaking its lustrous folds.

He was absorbed in this occupation when Robert entered.

"What do you think *you're* doing?"

"Oh, I jus' wanted to borrow a handkerchief, Robert. I thought you wun't mind lendin' me this handkerchief."

"Well, I would," said Robert curtly. "Give it back to me."

212

Reluctantly William handed it back to Robert.

"How much'll you give it me for?" he said.

"Well, how much have you?" said Robert, ruthlessly.

"Nothin' – jus' at present," admitted William. "But I'd *do* something for you for it. I'd do anythin' you want done for it. You just tell me what to do for it, an' I'll *do* it."

"Well, you can – you can get the Bishop's handkerchief for me, and then I'll give mine to you."

The trouble with Robert was that he imagined himself a wit.

The trouble with William was that he took things literally.

The Bishop was expected in the village the next day. It was the great event of the summer. He was a distant relation of the Vicar's.

He was to open the Fête, address a large meeting on Temperance, spend the night at the vicarage, and depart the next morning.

The Bishop was a fatherly, simple-minded old man of seventy. He enjoyed the Fête, except for one thing. Wherever he looked, he met the gaze of a freckled untidy frowning small boy.

He could not understand it. The boy seemed to be everywhere. The boy seemed to follow him about . . .

Then he addressed the meeting on Temperance, his audience consisting chiefly of adults. But in the front seat, the same earnest frowning boy fixed him with a determined gaze . . .

After the meeting William wandered down the road to the Vicarage. He pondered gloomily over his wasted afternoon. Fate had not thrown the Bishop's handkerchief in his path. But he did not yet despair.

He looked cautiously through the Vicarage hedge. Nothing was to be seen. He crawled inside the garden and round to the back of the house. The Bishop was tired after his address. He lay outstretched upon a deckchair beneath a tree.

Over the head and face of His Lordship, was stretched a large super-fine linen handkerchief. William's set expression brightened. On hands and knees he began to crawl through the grass, towards the portly form.

Crouching behind the chair, he braced himself for the crime; he measured the distance between the chair and the garden gate.

One, two, three – then suddenly the portly form stirred, the handkerchief was firmly withdrawn by a podgy hand, and a dignified voice yawned and said, "Heigh-ho!"

At the same moment the Bishop sat up. William, from his refuge behind the chair, looked wildly round. The door of the house was opening. There was only one thing to do.

William was as nimble as a monkey. Like a flash of lightning he disappeared up a tree. It was a very leafy tree. It completely concealed William, but William had a good bird's eye view of the world beneath him.

The Vicar came out rubbing his hands.

"You rested, my Lord?" he said.

"I'm afraid I've had forty winks," said His Lordship pleasantly. "Just dropped off, you know. I dreamt about that boy who was at the meeting this afternoon."

"What boy, my Lord?" asked the Vicar.

"I noticed him at the Fête and the meeting. He looked – he looked a soulful boy. I dare say you know him."

The Vicar considered.

"I can't think of any boy round here like that," he said.

The Bishop sighed.

"It seemed an earnest *questing* face – as if the boy wanted something – *needed* something. I hope my little talk helped him."

"Without doubt it did, my Lord," said the Vicar, politely. "I thought we might dine out here – the days draw out so pleasantly now."

The Vicar went to order dinner in the garden. The Bishop drew the delicate handkerchief once more over his rubicund features.

The breast of the Bishop on the lawn began to rise and sink. The figure of the Vicar was visible at the study window, as he gazed with fond pride upon the slumbers of his distinguished guest.

William dared not descend in view of that watching figure. Finally, it sat down in a chair by the window, and began to read a book.

William took from his pocket a bent pin attached to a piece of string. This apparatus lived permanently in his pocket, because he had not given up hope of catching a trout in the village stream.

He lowered this cautiously and drew the bent pin carefully on the white linen expanse.

Leaning down from his leafy retreat, William drew the bent pin sharply across. It missed the handkerchief and caught the Bishop's ear.

The Bishop sat up with a scream. William, pin and string withdrew into the shade of the branches.

The Vicar ran out from the house, full of concern.

"I've been badly stung in the ear by some insect," said the Bishop. "Some virulent tropical insect, I should think – very painful. Very painful indeed—"

"My Lord," said the Vicar. "I am so sorry – so very sorry – a thousand pardons – can I procure some remedy for you – vaseline, ammonia – er – cold cream—?"

"No, no, no, no," snapped the Bishop. "I put my handkerchief over my face for a protection. If I had failed to do that I should have been even more badly stung."

The Vicar sat himself down on his chair.

The maid came out to lay the table. They watched her in silence. William shifted his position in the tree.

"Do you know," said the Bishop, "I believe that there is a cat in the tree. Several times I have heard a slight rustling."

It would have been better for William to

remain silent, but William's genius occasionally misled him. He was anxious to prevent the investigation; to prove once and for all his identity as a cat.

He leant forward and uttered a re-echoing "Mi-*aw-aw-aw!*"

As imitations go, it was rather good.

There was a slight silence. Then, "It *is* a cat," said the Bishop in triumph.

"Excuse me, my Lord," said the Vicar.

He went softly into the house and returned holding a shoe.

"This will settle his feline majesty," he smiled.

Then he hurled the shoe violently into the tree.

"Sh! Scoot!" he said as he did it.

William was annoyed. The shoe narrowly missed his face. He secured it and waited.

"I hope you haven't lost the shoe," said the Bishop anxiously.

"Oh, no. The gardener's boy will get it for me."

He settled himself in his chair comfortably with a smile.

William leant down, held the shoe deliberately over the Vicar's bald head then dropped it.

"*Damn!*" said the Vicar. "Excuse me, my Lord."

"H'm," said the Bishop. "Er – yes – most annoying. It lodged in a branch for a time probably, and then obeyed the force of gravity."

The Vicar was rubbing his head. William wanted to enjoy the sight of the Vicar rubbing his head. He moved a little further along the branch.

He forgot all caution. There was the sound of a rending and a crashing, and on to the table between the amazed Vicar and Bishop descended William's branch and William.

The Bishop gazed at him. "Why, that's the boy," he said.

William sat up among the debris of broken glass and crockery. He discovered that he was

bruised and that his hand was cut by one of the broken glasses.

He extricated himself from the branch and the table, and stood rubbing his bruises and sucking his hand.

"Crumbs!" was all he said.

The Vicar was gazing at him speechlessly.

"You know, my boy," said the Bishop in mild reproach, "that's a very curious thing to do – to hide up there for the purpose of eavesdropping.

"I know that you are an earnest, well-meaning little boy, and that you were interested in my address this afternoon, and I dare say you were hoping to listen to me again, but this is my time for relaxation, you know.

"Suppose the Vicar and I had been talking about something we didn't want you to hear? I'm sure you wouldn't like to listen to things people didn't want you to hear, would you?"

William stared at him in unconcealed amazement.

The Vicar, with growing memories of shoes

and "damns" and with murder in his heart, was picking up twigs and broken glass.

He knew that he could not, in the Bishop's presence, say the things to William and do the things to William that he wanted to do and say.

He contented himself with saying, "You'd better go home now. Tell your father I'll be coming to see him tomorrow."

"A well-meaning little boy, I'm sure," said the Bishop kindly. "Well-meaning, but unwise – er – unwise. But your attentiveness during the meeting did you credit, my boy – did you credit."

William turned to go. He knew when he was beaten. He had spent a lot of time and trouble and had not secured the episcopal handkerchief. He had bruised himself and cut himself.

He understood the Vicar's veiled threat. He saw all his future pocket-money vanish into nothingness with the cost of the Vicar's glasses and plates.

He wouldn't have minded if he'd got the handkerchief. He wouldn't have minded anything if—

"Don't suck your hand, my boy," said the Bishop. "An open cut like that is most dangerous. Poison works into the system by it. You remember I told you how the poison of alcohol works into the system – well, any kind of poison can work into it by a cut – don't suck it; keep it covered up – haven't you a handkerchief? Here, take mine. You needn't trouble to return it. It's an old one."

The Bishop was deeply touched by what he called the "bright spirituality" of the smile with which William thanked him.

William, limping slightly, his hand covered by a grimy rag, came out into the garden, drawing from his pocket with a triumphant flourish an enormous, violently-coloured silk handkerchief.

Robert, who was weeding the rose-bed, looked up.

"Here," he called, "you can jolly well go and put that handkerchief of mine back."

William continued his proud advance.

"'S all right," he called airily, "the Bishop's is on your dressing-table."

Robert dropped his trowel.

"Gosh!" he gasped, and hastened indoors to investigate.

William went down to the gate, smiling very slightly.

"The days are drawing out so pleasantly," he was saying to himself in a mincing accent.

"Vaseline – ammonia – er – or cold cream. Damn!"

He leant over the gate and looked up and down the road. In the distance he caught sight of the figure of his friend.

"Gin-*ger*," he yelled in hideous shrillness.

He waved his coloured handkerchief carelessly in greeting as he called. Then he swaggered out into the road . . .

William and St Valentine

Miss Lomas held a Bible class for the Sons and Daughters of Gentlefolk every Tuesday afternoon after school. Something seemed to have happened to the class since William Brown joined it. The beautiful atmosphere was destroyed.

William took his seat in the dining-room where Miss Lomas always held her class. He took a large nut out of his pocket and cracked it with his teeth.

"*Not* in here, William," said Miss Lomas faintly.

"I was goin' to put the bits of shell into my

pocket," said William. "I wasn't goin' to put 'em on your carpet or anything; but 'f you don't want me to 's all right," he said obligingly, putting nut and dismembered shell into his pocket.

"Now," said Miss Lomas brightly, "I want to give you a little talk on Brotherly Love."

"Who's St Valentine?" said William who was burrowing in his prayer book.

"Why, William?" said Miss Lomas, patiently.

"Well, his day seems to be comin', this month," said William.

Miss Lomas, with a good deal of confusion, launched into a not very clear account of the institution of St Valentine's Day.

"Well, I don't think much of *him* 's a saint," was William's verdict, "writin' soppy letters to girls instead of gettin' martyred prop'ly like Peter an' the others."

Miss Lomas put her hand to her head.

"You misunderstand me, William," she said. "What I meant to say was . . . Well, suppose we leave St Valentine till later, and have our little talk on Brotherly Love first . . . *Ow-w-w!*"

The box containing William's pet stag-beetle, Albert, had accidentally opened in William's pocket, and Albert was now taking a voyage of discovery up Miss Lomas's jumper. Miss Lomas's spectacles fell off. She tore Albert off her and rushed from the room.

William gathered up his stag-beetle and carefully examined him.

"She might have hurt him, throwing him about like that," he said sternly. "She oughter be more careful."

Then he replaced Albert tenderly in his box.

At that moment, Miss Dobson entered the room. Miss Dobson was Miss Lomas's cousin and was staying with her. Miss Dobson was very young and very pretty. She had short golden curls and blue eyes and small white teeth and an attractive smile.

"My cousin's not well enough to finish the lesson," she said. "So, I'm going to read to you all till it's time to go home. Now, let's be comfortable. Come and sit on the hearthrug. That's right. I'm going to read to you 'Scalped by the Reds'."

At the end of the first chapter, William had decided that he wouldn't mind coming to this sort of Bible class every day.

At the end of the second he had decided to marry Miss Dobson as soon as he grew up . . .

*

When William woke up the next morning, his determination to marry Miss Dobson was unchanged.

He had previously agreed quite informally to marry Joan Parfitt, his friend and play-mate and adorer, but Joan was small and dark-haired and rather silent. She was not gloriously grown-up, and tall and fair and vivacious.

William was aware that marriage must be preceded by courtship, and that courtship was an arduous business.

It was a half-holiday that afternoon and, to the consternation of his family, William announced his intention of staying at home.

He knew that Laurence Hinlock, Ethel's latest admirer, was expected for tea and William wished to study at near quarters the delicate art of courtship.

He realised that he could not marry Miss Dobson for many years to come, but he did not see why his courtship of her should not begin at once . . . He was going to learn how it was done from Laurence Hinlock and Ethel . . .

He spent the earlier part of the afternoon collecting a few more insects for his empty boxes. (He was still mourning bitterly the loss of Albert, who had been confiscated that morning by the French master.)

Then he went indoors.

There were several people in the drawing-room. He greeted them rather coldly, his eye roving round the while for what he sought.

Ethel and a tall, lank young man were sitting in the window-alcove, in two comfortable chairs, talking vivaciously and confidentially.

William took a chair and carried it over to them, put it down by the young man's chair, and sat down.

There was a short, pregnant silence.

"Good afternoon," said William, at last.

"Er – good afternoon," said the young man.

There was another silence.

"Hadn't you better go and speak to the others?" said Ethel.

"I've spoke to them," said William.

Silence again.

"I think Mrs Franks would like you to go and talk to her," said Ethel.

"No, I don't think she would," said William with perfect truth.

The young man took out a shilling and handed it to William.

"Go and buy some sweets for yourself," he said.

William put the shilling in his pocket.

"Thanks," he said. "I'll go and get them when you've all gone."

There was another and yet deeper silence. Then Ethel and the young man began to talk together again.

They had evidently decided to ignore William's presence.

William listened with rapt attention. He wanted to know what you said and the sort of voice you said it in.

"St Valentine's Day next week," said Laurence soulfully.

"Oh, no one takes any notice of that nowadays," said Ethel.

"I'm going to," said Laurence. "I think it's a beautiful idea. Its meaning, you know . . . true love . . . If I send you a Valentine, will you accept it?"

"That depends on the Valentine," said Ethel with a smile.

"It's the thought that's behind it that's the vital thing," said Laurence. "It's that that mat-

236

ters. Ethel . . . you're in all my waking dreams."

"I'm sure I'm not," said Ethel.

"You are . . . Has anyone told you before that you're a perfect Botticelli?"

"Heaps of people," said Ethel calmly.

"I was thinking about love last night," said Laurence. "Love at first sight. That's the only sort of love . . . When I first saw you, my heart leapt at the sight of you."

Laurence was a great reader of romance.

"I think that we're predestined for each other. We must have known each other in former existences. We—"

"Do speak up," said William irritably. "You're speaking so low that I can't hear what you're saying . . ."

"What do people mean by sayin' they'll send a Valentine, Mother?" said William that evening. "I thought he was a sort of saint. I don' see how you can send a saint to anyone, 'specially when he's dead 'n' in the prayer book."

"Well, it's a kind of Christmas card," said Mrs Brown vaguely, "only it's a Valentine, I mean . . . well it had gone out in my day, but I remember your grandmother showing me some that had been sent to her . . . dried ferns and flowers pasted on cardboard . . . very pretty."

"Huh!" said William. "I don' see any sense in sendin' pasted ferns, an' dead saints and things . . . But still, I'm going to do all the sort of things they do."

"What *are* you talking about, William?" said Mrs Brown.

Interest in St Valentine's Day seemed to have infected the whole household. On February 13th, William came upon his brother Robert wrapping up a large box of chocolates.

"What's that?" said William.

"A Valentine," said Robert shortly.

"Well, Miss Lomas said it was a dead saint, and Mother said it was a pasted fern, an' now you start sayin' it's a box of chocolates! No

238

one seems to know what it is. Who's it for, anyway?"

"Doreen Dobson," said Robert, answering without thinking with a glorifying blush.

"Oh, I *say*!" said William indignantly. "You can't. I've bagged her. I'm going to do a fern for her. I've had her ever since Bible class."

"Shut up and get out," said Robert.

Robert was twice William's size. William shut up and got out.

*

The Lomas family was giving a party on Saint Valentine's Day and William had been invited with Robert and Ethel. William spent two hours on his Valentine.

He could not find a fern so he picked a large spray of yew-tree instead. He found a large piece of thick cardboard, about the size of a drawing-board, and a bottle of glue in the cupboard of his father's writing-desk.

It took the whole bottle of glue, plus some flour and water, to fix the spray of yew-tree to the cardboard, and the glue mingled freely with the flour and water on William's clothing and person.

Finally, he surveyed his handiwork.

"Well, I don't see much *in* it now it's done," he said. "But I'm jolly well going to do all the things they do."

He set off to Miss Lomas's carrying his Valentine under his arm. He started out before Ethel and Robert because he wanted to begin his courtship of Miss Dobson before anyone else was in the field.

Miss Lomas opened the door. She paled slightly as she saw William.

"You're rather early," she said.

"Yes, I thought I'd come early so's to be sure to be in time," said William. "Which room're we goin' to have tea in?"

With a gesture of hopelessness Miss Lomas showed him into the empty drawing-room.

"It's Miss Dobson I've really come for," explained William obligingly as he sat down.

Miss Lomas fled, but Miss Dobson did not appear.

William spent the interval wrestling with his Valentine. He had carried it sticky side towards his coat, and it now adhered closely to him.

He managed at last to tear it away, leaving a good deal of glue and bits of yew-tree still attached to the coat . . .

The guests began to arrive, Robert and Ethel among the first. Miss Dobson came in with Robert. He handed her a large box of chocolates.

"A Valentine," he said.

"Oh . . . thank you," said Miss Dobson, blushing.

William took up his enormous piece of gluey cardboard with bits of battered yew adhering at intervals.

"A Valentine," he said.

Miss Dobson looked at it in silence.

"W-what is it, William?" she said faintly.

"A Valentine," repeated William, annoyed at its reception.

"Oh," said Miss Dobson.

Robert led her over to the recess by the window, which contained two chairs. William followed, carrying his chair. He sat down beside them. Both ignored him.

"Quite a nice day, isn't it?" said Robert.

"Isn't it!" said Miss Dobson.

"Miss Dobson," said William, "I'm always dreamin' of you when I'm awake."

"What a pretty idea of yours to have a Valentine's Day party," said Robert.

"Do you think so?" said Miss Dobson coyly.

"Has anyone ever told you that you're like a bottled cherry?" said William doggedly.

"Do you know . . . this is the first Valentine I've ever given anyone?" said Robert.

"Oh . . . is it?" she said.

"I've been thinkin' about love at first sight," said William monotonously. "I got such a fright when I saw you first. I think we're pre-existed for each other. I—"

"Will you allow me to take you out in my side-car tomorrow?" said Robert.

"Oh, how lovely!" said Miss Dobson.

"No . . . predestinated . . . that's it," said William.

Neither of them took any notice of him. He felt depressed, and disillusioned. She wasn't much of a catch anyway. He didn't know why he'd even bothered about her.

He was quiet for a minute or two. Then he took up his Valentine which was lying on the floor, and walked out.

The Outlaws were in the old barn. They greeted William joyfully. Joan, the only girl member, was there with them. William handed her his cardboard.

"A Valentine," he said.

"A Valentine?" said Joan.

"Yes. Some say it's a saint what wrote soppy letters to girls an' some say it's a bit of fern like this an' some say it's a box of chocolates."

"Well, I never!" said Joan. "It's beautiful of you to give it to me, William."

"It's a jolly good piece of cardboard," said Ginger. "'F we scrape away these messy leaves an' stuff."

William joined with zest in the scraping.

"How's Albert?" said Joan.

After all, there was no one quite like Joan. He'd never contemplate marrying anyone else again.

"He's been took off me," said William.

"Oh, what a *shame*, William!"

"But I've got another . . . an earwig . . . called Fred."

"I'm so glad."

"But I like you better than *any* insect, Joan," he said generously.

"Oh, William, do you *really*?"

"Yes – an' I'm goin' to marry you when I grow up if you won't want me to talk a lot of soppy stuff that no one can understand."

"Oh, thank you, William . . . No, I won't."

"All right . . . now come on an' let's play Red Indians."